GW00866405

HARVEY RANGER

THE WHALE THAT WASN'T

STEPHEN W. SAINT

Cover illustration by Chris Macleod

Cover design by Pro EBookCovers

Interior layout design by Abdul Rehman

Copyright © 2021 by Stephen W. Saint

ISBN: 9798412585956 (Paperback)

Visit us on the web: HarveyRanger.com

AUTHOR'S NOTE

The story takes place in England and is written in British English. If you live in another country, the spelling of some words may differ from what you are familiar with. Punctuation and formatting are a blend of British and American style (some might call that Canadian).

Imperial measurements are still widely used in the United Kingdom (for example inches, miles, pounds), however the metric system has been used throughout this book. Harvey would have wanted it that way.

TABLE OF CONTENTS

ACKNOWLEDGEMENTS

Thanks to Paige, Roger, Shane, Maria, Emily, Ryan, Julia, Corbin, Emmett, Illana, Leslie, Felicity, Jesse, Grant, Esmé, Charlotte, Amelia, Jenny, Brodie, Celeste, Christa, Julia, and Isaac for taking the time to read various versions of this work. Without your feedback, encouragement, and suggestions, it's unlikely that I would have finished the job.

In addition to making various edits and corrections to an early draft of the book, Mr Schroeder pointed out that navy ships can't be readied for search missions in less than an hour. This criticism was pivotal in helping me take the story to a whole new level of drama and excitement, and for that I am very thankful.

While this is a work of fiction, I have tried to make everything as historically and scientifically accurate as possible. I would like to give a big shout-out to Catherine de Bertrand and members of the Dorset Dolphin Watch

Facebook group (Lucie, Sara, Lisa, and Jojo) for their collective memories of whale sightings on the Dorset coast over the past forty years. Catherine also took the time to read my book, make suggestions, and answer various questions for me. Thanks to Richard Samways, history consultant to the Weymouth Museum, for information on the Bincleaves site. And thanks to my dad, for documenting family stories from the Dorset area–these helped provide some of the historical context for this story.

Chris Macleod is a brilliant artist, and his cover art is amazing. If anyone buys this book, it'll probably be because of Chris. Thanks for taking a chance and working with me on this cover.

Despite my most excellent public school education, over the years I seem to have forgotten many of the basics of grammar. I would like to thank Kristen Lautenbach for editing, teaching, guiding, coaching, encouraging, and mentoring me throughout the process of creating this book. Your support was invaluable. Also thanks to my sister, Helen Saint Kelly, for her edits and corrections.

Thanks to my mum for telling me stories when I was a small boy, and for creating amazing picture books for your grandchildren. You helped instil in me a passion for storytelling.

Thanks to my daughters for inspiring me to tell bedtime stories, and for providing great fodder for the characters of Harvey and Sally. Thanks to my lovely wife, Kay, for encouraging me throughout the process and putting up with me taking time away from real life to work on this (although there were many times you probably thought I was doing real work when I was actually working on this project–sorry about that.) By the way, in case you didn't know, you're Mrs Ranger.

Finally and most importantly, I want to thank my Creator, the originator of all creativity. In Him I live and move and have my being.

For Bellsie and Soph

Above all else, guard your heart,
for everything you do flows from it.
(Proverbs 4:23)

Chapter 1

THE HUMPBACK OF PORTLAND BILL

Overlooking the English Channel and just a ten-minute walk from the town centre of Weymouth stood an old stone house. It was large and grey and made from the same limestone as Buckingham Palace. In the house lived an eleven-year-old boy named Harvey, the middle child of Reginald and Olivia Ranger.

Of the three Ranger children, Harvey was the one you would least expect to do anything newsworthy, the one least likely to have his exploits recorded in the annals of history. He was less outgoing than his older brother Jack and much quieter than his rambunctious younger sister Sally. Yet despite Harvey's placid demeanour, adventure and excitement entered his young life far more often than you might expect.

You see, Harvey was the owner of a small fleet of drones. The less expensive drones, Harvey had purchased himself after helping with Jack's lawn-care business and doing photography for his Aunt Jenny, who sold houses. The more high-tech drones had been given to Harvey as thank-you gifts from various people who had benefited from his actions with one of his flying machines.

Aunt Jenny should probably be thanked as well, since she was the one who inspired Harvey's interest in drones. One day, when Harvey was nine years old, his aunt had handed him a camera bag containing a Nikon SLR camera and several lenses. "Here," she said. "I never got past the 'P' mode. If you can figure it out, you can keep it and pay me back by taking photos for my listings."

Harvey had quickly taught himself the basics of photography and was soon capable of capturing fine images of the properties his aunt needed to sell. Around that time, other estate agents had just begun using drones to capture aerial images of their listings. Aunt Jenny did not want to be left behind, so in consultation with Harvey (who researched the matter thoroughly), she purchased a drone of her own, one featuring a 12-megapixel telephoto zoom camera. One thing led to another, and it wasn't long before most of Harvey's spare time involved the use of drones.

But time had passed, and, as happens with many fun and exciting things, Harvey was experiencing what economists refer to as the law of diminishing returns. He'd had many adventures with his drones and had managed to build a respectable video library of the coastline within cycling distance of his home. He'd captured video of the occasional dolphin and even had some grainy footage of what he was convinced was a giant sea turtle. But Harvey yearned for more, for another way he could use his drones, for some other direction in which he could point his eye in the sky.

★ ★ ★

It was a Thursday evening in mid-September. Harvey was sitting on the sofa beside his seven-year-old sister, Sally, while she read out loud to him from her level nine Biff and Chip home reading book, *The Princes in the Tower*. Mr Ranger reclined on the other end of the sofa next to Sally, with his feet on an ottoman and his hands behind his head. Mrs Ranger sat in a comfy armchair, sipping chai tea. The two adults were taking in the tranquillity of the moment and enjoying the sound of their youngest child reading while Harvey helped Sally with the more challenging words.

"I'm glad the boys were able to escape from the tower," Sally remarked as she finished the last page.

"And that was really clever of Biff," said Harvey, "to think of tying their bedsheets together to make the guards believe they'd escaped out the window, and then sneaking out the open door when the guards left to chase them."

"Mum," asked Sally, "would that story be in the news if it happened today?"

Harvey jumped in before Mrs Ranger could answer. "It's just fiction, Sally. It's all made up."

"Actually," Mrs Ranger corrected Harvey, "it's not all made up. There were once two princes held in the Tower of London. It just didn't end as well for them as it did for the princes in the Biff and Chip book." She smiled at Sally. "And yes, it would be front-page news if it happened today."

"So, what *really* happened to them?" Harvey asked.

Mrs Ranger dodged the question. "Oh look, it's time for the news!" she exclaimed. When Sally wasn't looking, she caught Harvey's attention and mouthed the words *I'll tell you later.*

Mr Ranger picked up the remote and turned on the television to watch the local news. First, there was a story about a woman who needed to be rescued after becoming stuck up to her waist in the mud, and then came one about a cat from Charminster that had turned up in Scotland after being missing for six months. The TV showed a clip of the cat and its owner being reunited before going to a toothpaste commercial.

"I used to think the news was incredibly boring," Harvey commented. "But after being in the news myself a few times, I find it more interesting."

"It's not just that," said his mum. "You're growing up. It's only natural for you to start to care more about things other than yourself."

The commercial finished, and they turned their attention back towards the TV.

"That's annoying," said Harvey as the news resumed. "That video is shot with a phone held vertically. Why do people do that? Don't they know they can turn their phones ninety degrees? We pay good money for televisions that are in landscape mode, and then other people go and waste all that lovely screen space by shooting lousy videos in portrait mode. There should be a law against it." He paused for a breath. "What is that thing, anyway? It just looks like a big blurry black blob in the sea."

"Harvey, if you will just be quiet for a moment, we'll find out," said his dad.

Harvey stopped talking and listened to the reporter.

"...and we'd like to thank Mary Bunt of Fortuneswell for this video footage of the humpback whale she spotted near Portland Bill this morning."

Harvey turned to his parents. "I had no idea that whales could be found anywhere near here. Did you know there were whales 'round here?"

"I did," replied his mum. "But I've never actually seen one myself."

"I saw a humpback when I was in my twenties," said Mr Ranger. "I was able to follow it along the coast between Weymouth and Swanage."

"So they're pretty rare," said Harvey. "Does that mean if I get some nice close-up video of this humpback, I might be in the news again?"

"It's not fair if you get to be in the news again," Sally whined. "You've been in the news lots of times, and I've never been in the news once."

"Oh, don't be jealous about that," Mrs Ranger smiled. "Fame and glory aren't all they're cracked up to be. Sometimes, it's better to fly under the radar and not be noticed. I know I wouldn't want to be famous. Anonymity is a precious thing."

"How would you know?" Harvey interjected. "You've never been famous."

"That's true, I haven't. But I once heard someone famous say that, and it makes sense to me."

"Well, *I'd* like to be famous," insisted Harvey. "But it's not so much about *being* famous as it is about the challenge of it, like climbing a mountain just because the mountain is there."

"You've already climbed the mountain!" Sally protested. "Now it's my turn. I want to be in the news."

"But the mountain's still there," said Harvey, "and I want to climb it again. Nothing's stopping you from climbing your own mountain."

Mrs Ranger turned to Harvey again. "If they played that blurry whale video from Mary Bunt, I'm pretty sure some high-quality Harvey Ranger footage would be newsworthy. And if you caught that whale breaching, you might just get on the front page of the BBC."

"That would be amazing. Too bad I've got school tomorrow. By the time I get home, it'll be starting to get dark. Otherwise, I could've biked over to Portland. What are the chances the whale will still be hanging around on Saturday?"

"I'm not exactly a whale expert, but I'm thinking it might stick around for a while if there's enough to eat,"

Mrs Ranger reasoned. "Your best bet for finding any animal is to learn as much as you can about its habits. What does it like to eat? Where and how does it sleep?" She looked at the clock. "Screen time's done for this evening," she announced, turning off the TV. "But you could always look up *whales* in..."

She was going to say "Grandma's old encyclopaedia set," but she didn't have to. Harvey was already on his feet and pulling down *Funk & Wagnalls Encyclopaedia Volume 27* with *Vermo to World* written on the spine.

Encyclopaedia in hand, Harvey ran upstairs to get ready for bed.

★ ★ ★

Having completed his usual bedtime routine, Harvey sat up in bed, opened Funk & Wagnalls, and turned to the section on whales. He read that humpback whales grew to a length of sixteen metres and weighed as much as 36,000 kilograms. He was pleased to learn that there were a lot more humpbacks now than there had been in the past, when they'd been hunted to near extinction.

It wasn't just hunting that posed a threat to whales. The article explained that whales sometimes got caught up in fishing nets. Pair trawlers, which are two fishing boats that drag a net between them, were a big part of the problem. Dolphins, which the encyclopaedia explained were a type of toothed whale, became caught in the nets more often than humpbacks. *That's strange,* Harvey thought. *I've never thought of dolphins as a type of whale.*

The topic of dolphins reminded Harvey of something his best friend, James Buckeridge, had told him a couple of weeks prior. James had a sister named Wendy, who was fifteen years older and a marine biologist–a fact James liked to mention on a regular basis. Wendy occasionally led groups of volunteers on boat trips where they would count the dolphins and other marine animals they observed in and around Weymouth Bay. If Harvey was recalling the information correctly, the next trip was this Saturday, and on this trip the boat would be going out past Portland Bill. The idea of going on the trip had appealed to Harvey at first, but when he'd learned of the twenty-pound cost he'd put it out of his mind. Now, the ticket price didn't seem so bad. He decided he would ask James about it when he saw him at school in the morning.

When Harvey finally turned off the light and lay his head on the pillow, he imagined he was standing near the Portland lighthouse. He was wearing the first-person view drone goggles that allowed him to see exactly what the drone's camera was viewing. He pictured flying out over the water. Immediately in front of him, a massive humpback whale was jumping clear out of the sea, and Harvey was capturing it all in beautiful, high-resolution video and stunning stills with the drone's 20-megapixel camera. The last mental picture he had before drifting off to sleep was of a National Geographic magazine cover with a photo of an airborne humpback. The caption at the bottom read *Photography by Harvey Ranger.*

Chapter 2

THE BANOFFEE DEAL

O n Friday morning, after a night of dreaming about an evil whale that shot down drones with its blowhole and his mother becoming famous for some unknown reason, Harvey swung his legs over the side of the bed and sat up. He looked across the room, where his brother Jack's bed was empty, as was the spot on the floor where Jack's scruffy, grey-haired dog, Radar, usually slept. Normally, if Jack left early, Radar would return to wait for Harvey. As Harvey sat contemplating the likelihood that he'd be able to join James for tomorrow's boat tour, he smelled the reason for Radar's absence. *Sausages*. Hungry as always, Harvey headed downstairs to the kitchen.

Radar was standing as close to the sausages as he could get with his head up, tongue out, and eyes pleading. Mrs Ranger was by the stove, looking stylish in a black skirt, white t-shirt, denim jacket, and a pair of sunglasses perched on top of her head. Mrs Ranger always looked stylish, especially now that fashion had become her current *thing*. Previously it had been juicing, and before that it was knitting. Her newfound passion had even prompted her to start a wardrobe consulting business called Wardrobe OR, short for Wardrobe Operating Room.

Mrs Ranger looked up as Harvey walked in. "Morning, love," she said. "Before Dad left this morning, he cooked up some quiche and sausages for us." She placed a plate on the table in front of Harvey. "Dad also left you some treats from Auntie's to take to school," she added, pointing to a white box on the counter.

The side of the box said *Auntie Bunny's*, which was the name of the bakery owned by Mr Ranger. In the Ranger home, the bakery was always referred to as just Auntie's. Since Mr Ranger prided himself in guaranteeing the freshness of the merchandise at Auntie's, the not-so-fresh (but still quite delicious) treats often made their way back to the Ranger home.

"The treats are to share," Mrs Ranger continued. "You've got eclairs. You've got chocolate chip cookies, and you've got banoffee squares in there…"

"Rectangles!" Harvey interjected.

"What about rectangles?"

"They're rectangles, not squares. Dad never cuts them into squares. I doubt that anyone in the history of the world has ever cut them into actual squares, so they should really be called rectangles."

Mrs Ranger rolled her eyes.

Harvey was a frequent witness to eye-rolling. It happened a lot around him due to his unique passion for details, facts, and literal interpretations of figures of speech. He had a penchant for applying these passions in a somewhat cheeky manner, partly for his own entertainment and partly because he, at times, genuinely thought that his interpretations were valid and ought to be appreciated. There was no debating team at Weybourne College where Harvey attended, but had there been, Harvey would almost certainly have been the team captain.

"If you're going to get all technical about it, then you'll need to call them *banoffee rectangular prisms*," Mrs Ranger replied. "But whatever you choose to call them, there's enough sugar in the box to guarantee your popularity until at least the end of today." She smiled slyly. It wasn't often that someone one-upped Harvey, and she derived a certain amount of pleasure from the victory.

Harvey quietly devoured his four sausages and three slices of quiche before loading his empty plate into the dishwasher. "Thanks, Mum," he said, hugging his mother. She kissed him on the cheek and handed him the box of treats. Harvey bent down to rearrange the contents of his backpack, making sure there was enough room for the precious cargo. With the goods safely stowed, he stood up to leave. "Bye, Mum!" he announced.

"Hold on a second. Have you brushed your teeth?" asked Mrs Ranger.

"Yes," Harvey answered, with a sheepish grin.

Mrs Ranger knew that look. It meant, *I'm not lying, but I might be misleading you.* "Today, Harvey? Have you brushed your teeth today?"

"No, it wasn't actually today. You asked me if I'd brushed my teeth, and I've brushed my teeth literally thousands of times."

Harvey went back up the stairs and brushed his teeth before hugging his mother a second time and heading out the door.

★ ★ ★

After six minutes of mostly uphill riding, Harvey turned right into Mulberry Lane and coasted his bicycle down the lane past Rodwell Retirement Lodge. His Uncle Denny was in the garden, pruning some roses. He was the proud owner of the lodge and always kept the property in pristine condition. Of all his uncles, it was Uncle Denny who most understood Harvey and the two shared a special bond, but Harvey had no time to chat today.

Still somewhat out of breath from the ride, Harvey slowed down as he approached the end of the lane. Mulberry Lane was a cul-de-sac, at the end of which the imposing three-storey, stone building of Weybourne College had stood facing northeast since the year 1709. The structure consisted of the main centre building and two smaller wings, which together formed three sides of a rectangle. The fourth side of the rectangle was completed by the tennis courts, visitor car park, and bike shed. It was into this shed that Harvey rode his bike and placed it in the rack.

"James," Harvey called out as he snapped his bike lock shut and ran to catch up with his best friend. "Is Wendy doing that whale-watching trip tomorrow?"

"Wendy doesn't organize whale-watching trips. They're mostly for dolphin spotting. I suppose if she spotted a whale, then you could call it a whale-watching trip."

"Same thing," Harvey said. "Dolphins are a type of toothed whale. I read it in the encyclopaedia last night."

"No, it's not the same thing. They're *toothed* whales, but they're still not whales. I should know, Wendy is a marine biologist."

"My dad's a baker, but that doesn't mean I know how to make chocolate eclairs."

"That's a really good point. And your mum's a wardrobe consultant, but that doesn't mean you know how to dress yourself."

Harvey used his fifteen-centimetre height advantage to put James in a playful headlock. "And my brother's a wrestling champion, and he taught me to do this."

"Okay, okay," laughed James. "Let's assume you're able to dress yourself. But why do you want to know about the trip?"

"I've changed my mind about coming. If you can get me on that boat, I'll give you a banoffee square." Harvey knew his friend was rather partial to the gooey, banana-flavoured treats.

"Deal," James smiled. "You can go on the trip."

Harvey released his grip from around James' neck to open the door of the school for him. "What do you mean, *deal*? You haven't even talked to Wendy yet."

"Don't need to. Wendy called me last night to say there were a couple of tickets left and to see if I wanted to go. She said I could bring a friend. By *friend* I think she meant you, and by *you* I think she meant you and one of your drones."

"Really? Why do you think she meant me?"

"Because she said, 'You can bring a friend, and if that friend is Harvey and he brings a drone, you can both ride for free.'" James smiled triumphantly. "I tricked you. And you still owe me a banoffee square."

"On the contrary," Harvey smirked, "I tricked *you*. I've got a whole box of treats, and I was going to give you a couple of banoffee squares anyway."

Chapter 3

THE NO-SHOW

"Good morning Harvey it's oh-seven-hundred hours on Saturday morning," said Alexa, his personal electronic assistant. Harvey had set Alexa to use the twenty-four hour clock. This meant that 7:00 a.m. was oh-seven-hundred-hours and 1:00 p.m. was thirteen-hundred-hours. The electronic assistant continued, "It's currently fourteen degrees centigrade and overcast. You have a whale-watching trip this morning at oh-eight-hundred hours."

Jack rolled over in bed. "Alexa, stop," he moaned. "Harvey, wasn't your vibrating watch enough to wake you up?"

"Sorry, sometimes I sleep through it. This trip is too important to miss. Besides, you're usually up way before me."

"Yeah, well that's why I'm sleeping in today. At least, I was going to sleep in, until you ruined it."

Harvey climbed out of bed and grabbed his basket of dirty laundry before heading downstairs.

In the kitchen, his mum was unloading the washing machine. "You can set your clothes there on the floor, and I'll load them for you,'" she said. "We're having porridge with mashed banana this morning, so help yourself from the pot on the stove."

Sally had just finished eating and was getting up from the table. "I'll get it for you," she said. "I added sprinkles and marshmallows to mine. It was delicious. Would you like me to add some toppings to yours?"

"Yeah, that would be great," Harvey said, and then remembering her track record added, "Just not too much."

Sally ladled a bowl of porridge for Harvey, added some whipped cream, and made a smiley face out of chocolate chips. She placed the bowl in front of Harvey.

"Thanks, Sal. That looks very creative. I'm sure this is going to be delicious."

"Speaking of creativity," said Mrs Ranger, "Dad had one of those last-minute creative urges he gets from time to time and has gone on one of his little painting holidays.

23

It'll be a short one this time. He said he'd be back later this afternoon."

"I don't know why he bothers," Harvey said. "If you see a scene you like, it's so much quicker to take a photo than to paint it. Painting is messy and such a waste of time."

"Well, he enjoys having a way to express himself artistically."

"Not sure why. Doesn't he get to be creative at work with the cakes and stuff? Anyway, it's strange how his desire to be creative always seems to come on at the last minute."

"Carpe diem, Harvey," said Mrs Ranger.

"He's going fishing for carp as well?"

Mrs Ranger smiled. "Your gran pays thousands of pounds a year for you to go to a posh private school to learn basic Latin. I know perfectly well you know that means *seize the day*."

Harvey scooped another spoonful of porridge into his mouth while Mrs Ranger loaded the last of Harvey's clothes into the washing machine. "Did you forget your pyjamas? I didn't see any pyjamas in there."

"No, I didn't forget them. I've decided that my clothes are comfortable enough to sleep in, and that sleeping in my clothes will save me a lot of time in the morning *and* save the environment."

"How does sleeping in your clothes save the environment?"

"Think of all the water that's wasted by people washing pyjamas. And think about all the pollution that's spewed into the environment by all the pyjama factories around the world. Anyone who says they care about the environment and wears pyjamas is a hypocrite."

"You might have a point," his mum agreed. "Reducing consumption is the best way to protect the environment."

Having finished his porridge, Harvey grabbed his backpack, hugged his mum goodbye, and hopped on his bike.

* * *

Five minutes later, Harvey arrived at Weymouth Harbour and pulled up to a stop beside an orange and white twin-hull boat with *Sidon* and *Carters Charters* printed on the side.

"Mornin', lad," called out Carter Rhodes himself from the deck of the boat. "I'm just gettin' everything ship-shape for a private tour this morning. What brings you this way?"

"If you're talking about the tour organised by Wendy Buckeridge, then I'm going to be joining you," said Harvey. "James, her brother, told me there were a couple of extra spaces for us."

"Always an extra spot for you, Master Ranger," said Carter. "Why don't you come aboard?"

Harvey locked his bike to an old iron guard rail and headed down the gangplank onto the deck of the *Sidon*. He set his backpack down gently on one of the benches in the centre of the deck.

Carter eyed the backpack. "Ya got one of your drones in there, lad?"

"Yeah, it's my Buzzbird 400, with the folding arms. I was hoping to use it today, if that's okay with you. I'd like to get some video of the humpback that was spotted on Thursday."

"So you heard about that, did ya? News spreads fast in this town. Rare sightin', that. Not many whales 'round these parts. Couple of minkes spotted up by Swanage a few years back, but not since eighty-six have I heard tell of a humpback. Wouldn't place much hope in spottin' that fella today. Likely moved on by now. Hopefully some dolphins, but a humpback...that would be somethin' special, that would." He turned and opened the door to the wheelhouse. "Come on in, and we'll put the kettle on in case anyone wants a cuppa."

Harvey watched as Carter puttered around in the wheelhouse, getting tea and coffee ready for the trip. During the summer, Harvey had helped Carter expand his fishing business by using one of his drones to carry Carter's clients' lures hundreds of metres out to sea. This work had always been from the shore at Chesil Beach. He'd never been aboard the *Sidon* before, and the array of gadgets and gauges mounted on the console fascinated him.

"We've got GPS, Sonar, VHF radio and radar. Fishin' ain't what it used to be in the ole days. It's all technology now," Carter explained. "We could spot a minnow at the bottom of the Mariana Trench with this one." He pointed to a device mounted on top of the console with a screen the size of a small tablet. "That's the sonar display. Do ya know how sonar works?"

Harvey nodded. "It's connected to a transducer in the water. The transducer emits pulses of sound and then measures the sound waves as they're bounced back. I've got sonar on one of my drones."

"Doesn't surprise me, lad. You seem to have a drone for every occasion."

Harvey grinned. "I don't think my drone would be able to spot a minnow in the Mariana Trench."

Out of the corner of his eye, Harvey saw James coming down the gangplank with Wendy. He stood to open the door of the wheelhouse.

"Morning, Harvey," said Wendy. "I'm glad you could come. James mentioned you were wanting to search for whales with your drone."

"That's right. But Carter said I shouldn't hope for much."

"Well, Carter's right. But hopefully we'll at least see Danny."

"Who's Danny?" Harvey asked.

"His full name is Danny the Dorset Dolphin. He's a large, adult male bottlenose. He's been a regular around these parts for a couple of weeks."

* * *

By 7:55 a.m., most of the volunteer dolphin spotters had arrived. There was a family of four with two curly-haired girls, a friend of Wendy's, two ladies Harvey recognised as helpers from the homeless centre where his mother frequently volunteered, and a very stocky man whom Harvey thought would have made an excellent rugby player. The only person who hadn't arrived yet was a woman by the name of Miss Gale.

They were still waiting for Miss Gale to show up when a tall man with thick ginger hair and a bushy beard stepped onto the gangplank.

"Good morning," Wendy called out. "Can I help you?"

"I was hoping ya might still have rrroom fer me on yer wee boat," said the man in a deep and raspy Scottish accent.

"So sorry, we're all booked up," Wendy apologised. "But if you don't mind waiting around for a few minutes, you can come with us if there's a no-show." She looked down at her watch. It was nearly 8:00 a.m., and Miss Gale still hadn't arrived.

Wendy knew Miss Gale quite well, as she had attended all the previous dolphin counts as far back as Wendy could remember. A sprightly seventy-eight-year-old, Miss Gale was never late for anything. Wendy was surprised that she wasn't there already.

"That would be just dandy," the man agreed. "I don't mind holding my horses fer a wee bit."

Harvey watched as the man walked back up the gangplank and sat on a bench. He couldn't help thinking that there was something familiar about the man, but he couldn't figure out what it was.

James leaned over and spoke quietly in Harvey's ear. "He looks like a ginger Santa Claus."

"He sure does. He's even more ginger than you. And the man behind you is so stocky, he reminds me of a tank."

"Shall we call one the Ginger Santa and the other, the Tank?" James whispered.

Harvey nodded, smiling.

It was now precisely 8:00 a.m., so Wendy pulled out her phone and rang up Miss Gale. "Oh dear," Wendy said into the phone. "Sorry to hear that...hopefully next time." She slipped the phone back into her pocket.

"Her bicycle has a puncture," Wendy explained to the group. "She doesn't want to hold us up and said we should go on ahead." Wendy waved to the Ginger Santa. "You can come aboard," she called. "One person will not be coming."

The man walked down the gangplank and handed Wendy a twenty-pound note before sitting down on a bench next to the Tank.

Chapter 4

DOLPHINS AREN'T WHALES

After providing a safety briefing, Carter fired up the twin diesel engines and carefully navigated his ten-metre boat towards the entrance of the harbour.

"What's that building over there?" asked the Tank.

"That's Nothe Fort," Wendy answered. "Construction on the fort was completed in 1872 to protect Weymouth Harbour. The fort closed in 1961. These days, it's a museum."

"Sorry, I'm a bit deaf in my left ear," the Tank spoke up. "Did you say it was still in use as a fort today?" He turned his head to the left so his right ear would be closer to Wendy.

"No," Wendy spoke louder. "The fort closed in 1961. It's a museum now."

"It's shaped like a letter *D* if you look at it from above," Harvey piped up. He was standing to the Tank's right, so he didn't have to repeat himself. "I've seen it from the air many times. There were four anti-aircraft guns placed there during World War II. Look, you can still see three of them sticking out." He pointed to where the guns jutted out at the top of the wall.

"Thank you, Harvey," said Wendy before she continued. "In a moment, we're going to be turning right and heading south towards Portland Harbour. It's a massive harbour that includes the entire southeast end of Weymouth Bay. The harbour is naturally protected by the island of Portland on the south side, Chesil Beach on the west, and Weymouth to the north. Carter told me that most sightings of Danny the Dolphin have been inside Portland Harbour, so keep your eyes peeled."

The group searched the water intently as the boat exited Weymouth Harbour and turned south towards the northernmost entrance to Portland Harbour.

"What are those buildings used for?" asked the Tank, pointing towards the breakwater.

"Those buildings, and the group of buildings on the shore at the end of the breakwater, were used during the war for testing torpedoes. They're all derelict now. No one uses them for anything."

"That's very interesting," the Tank said. "Very interesting indeed."

"My dad told me the breakwater is called Bincleaves Groyne," said Harvey. "And that at one time, they were also working on sonar in those buildings."

"Harvey, I'm really glad you came along. You're a wealth of information," Wendy smiled.

Carter piloted the boat around the southern end of Bincleaves Groyne and entered Portland Harbour. All eyes were scanning the water for signs of a dolphin.

James leaned against the gunwale, next to Harvey. "I really hope we see at least one dolphin today," he said.

"Yeah, that would be brilliant," Harvey agreed. "Then we'll be able to tell everyone we saw a whale in Weymouth Bay."

"I told you yesterday that dolphins aren't whales," James said, giving Harvey a playful knock on the head.

Wendy overheard them and joined the conversation. "Technically, Harvey is right *and* wrong. It depends on how you define the term *whale*. You see, all whales, dolphins, and porpoises are called *cetaceans*. There are two types of cetaceans, baleen whales and toothed whales. The dolphin is a toothed whale."

"Told ya," said Harvey. "If a dolphin is a toothed whale, then it's a whale."

"Hold on," said Wendy. "Like I said, it depends what you mean by the word whale. When scientists use the term *whale* by itself, they're typically referring to all cetaceans *except* dolphins, even though dolphins are toothed whales. It's a bit confusing, but that's the way it is."

"Alright," Harvey acquiesced. "If we spot a dolphin, then at least I can say I spotted a *toothed* whale. What if we spot a killer whale?"

"Killer whales are dolphins," said James, who had absorbed much of his sister's knowledge.

"That's true," said Wendy. "But it depends on what you mean by the word *dolphin*. Scientifically speaking, killer whales are dolphins, and that means they aren't whales. However, when most people talk about dolphins, they're referring to a cetacean that has *dolphin* in its name, like the bottlenose dolphin or striped dolphin. They wouldn't say, 'Oh look, there's a dolphin!' if they saw a killer whale, because that would be confusing."

Everyone kept their eyes peeled on the water while they pondered this information. They all wanted to be the first to spot a cetacean of *any* kind.

Harvey broke the silence. "So, let me get this straight. Dolphins are toothed whales, but they *aren't* whales because scientists say they aren't. And killer whales aren't whales because they're actually dolphins, but you can't call a killer whale a dolphin or that would confuse people.

Well, I'm not like most people. If we see a killer whale today, I'm going to make a point of saying, 'Oh look, there's a dolphin!'"

James smiled slyly. "You're right about one thing, Harvey," he said. "You're not like most people."

Chapter 5

OLIVIA THE DORSET MUM

The *Sidon* was now nearing the south end of Portland Harbour. There had been no sightings of any whales or dolphins, or any other type of cetacean. Carter stopped the boat and exited the wheelhouse. "We're going to be leaving the Portland Harbour in a minute," he said. "It's going to be choppier than it is here in the harbour. If any of you are prone to motion sickness, we have some ginger for you to chew on." He held up a plastic container in one hand. "And just in case the ginger doesn't work, we have these." He held up some sick bags in his other hand. "And don't forget to keep your eyes on the horizon."

"Thanks, Carter," said Wendy. "And before we go on, I thought we should do something that I should have done at the beginning. Let's all go around and introduce ourselves. I'll start. I'm Wendy Buckeridge," she began.

"I'm the president of the local chapter of the Organization for Recording Cetaceous Observations, more commonly known as ORCO." She turned around to show them the back of her blue coat, which had *ORCO* embroidered in large letters. "And, in case you haven't already guessed, I'm the organiser for this event." She turned and looked at James, who was next.

"I'm James Buckeridge," he said, "and I'm Wendy's younger brother."

James turned to Harvey, who stood beside him. Harvey started to introduce himself, "And I'm Harvey..."

Before Harvey could state that his surname was Ranger, he was interrupted by the Ginger Santa.

"Look over there!" hollered the man, while pointing back in the direction they had just come. "Did I just see a dorsal fin sticking out of the water?"

The others came to look.

"Over there, by that flock of seagulls!" The Ginger Santa pointed in the direction of the shore.

"We often see seagulls around dolphins," Carter explained. "They like to fish together." Carter joined the rest of the volunteers, who were now looking north towards the swooping gulls. "And if there was just one dorsal fin, it was almost certainly Danny. He's a big fella.

Probably because he doesn't have to share the fish he catches with anyone else."

Everyone had binoculars except for Harvey. "Do you see anything, James?" he asked as he sidled up beside his friend.

"Just a bunch of gulls swooping around like dive bombers, but nothing that looks like it might be cetaceous."

"Is that even a word?"

"Yes, it's a word. It's the C in ORCO, you numbskull. It means anything that's a cetacean."

"Well, Mr Know-it-All. Maybe you could tell us how long a bottlenose dolphin can hold its breath?"

James hesitated, so Wendy jumped in. "Good to see you boys getting along so well. A dolphin can hold its breath for ten minutes, so he *could* still be there. It would also be easy to miss him at this distance, if he came up for air." She turned to Carter. "We'll need to go back and investigate, if we're going to confirm the sighting."

"That would be a two-kilometre round trip if we did go back," Carter said. He didn't look too happy about the prospect of doubling back the way they had just come.

"I could send my drone," Harvey offered. "That would be a lot quicker."

Carter looked pleased. The extra fuel costs would have cut into his narrow profit margin, and the drone would save money as well as time. "Great idea, Harvey. We'll hold our position here and wait for you to do some reconnaissance."

Harvey removed his Buzzbird 400 from its case and placed it on the deck away from the other volunteers. For storage, the arms and propellers had been folded against the main body, so Harvey carefully unfolded them. With the drone ready to go, he removed the controller and FPV goggles from the case. Flying with the goggles on was like actually being in the pilot's seat of the drone.

With everything unpacked and ready to go, Harvey powered on the goggles, controller, and drone. He waited until he heard a loud beep coming from the drone. This told him that the GPS signal had been locked in and that the drone knew where it was in the world. Harvey then pulled the FPV goggles over his eyes, and with a push forward on the controller's right stick, he launched the drone into the air.

Harvey had flown his drones on many occasions, but he had never lost the thrilling feeling of actually being in the drone. He stopped for a moment, looking back at the boat. "Group shot," he called out. "Everyone wave!" He pressed a button on the controller to capture a photo of the group waving at him before turning and heading back towards the mainland.

Sixty seconds after leaving the *Sidon*, the drone arrived over the location where the seagulls were fishing. The gulls scattered with the arrival of the drone. As the last one flew off, Harvey positioned the drone directly over the area where they had been fishing. "I've arrived at the spot," he said.

"Can you see anything?" asked the Tank. Harvey couldn't see the Tank's face, but he sensed that he was quite excited.

"Sorry, I can't see anything yet," Harvey said. "I'll go higher, so I can see a wider area."

"Anything now?" asked the Tank after a minute.

"Sorry," said Harvey again, "there doesn't seem to be anything there."

"Thanks for trying, Harvey," said Carter. "You just saved us a whole bunch of time."

Before returning to the *Sidon*, Harvey turned the camera toward his own house, which was just a few hundred metres away. He spotted some movement in his back garden. "Hang on a sec," said Harvey with mock excitement. "I think I see something."

"What is it? What do you see?" Wendy said.

"It's a large adult mammal," said Harvey, "and it's got teeth."

"I bet it's Danny the Dorset Dolphin!" said the Tank.

"No, it's not Danny," said Harvey. "It's a female."

"How do you know it's a female?" asked James.

"I dunno. I just do," Harvey replied.

"Harvey, you wouldn't be able to tell if it was male or female from this distance," said Wendy. "It's most likely Danny."

"No, it's not Danny," Harvey grinned. "It's Olivia."

"Olivia!" responded several of the volunteers in surprise.

"Why Olivia?" asked James.

"Because," said Harvey, "it's Olivia, my Dorset mum. She's in our back garden, hanging my pants on the line to dry."

Moans erupted from the group, and Harvey thought about how helpful it would be if he could hand out some treats from Auntie's. Unfortunately, he hadn't brought any, so he realised he would have to restore his social standing on the boat by some other means.

"Well, laddie," said the Ginger Santa, interrupting Harvey's thoughts. "You be a good boy this afternoon and help your mother oot by taking those things down off the line."

Chapter 6

THE MEGA POD

With the drone safely back on board, Carter opened up the throttle and piloted the boat through the southernmost gap in the breakwater and towards the open sea.

"Sorry you haven't spotted a whale yet, Harvey," said Wendy as the boat continued on, past the Island of Portland. "As far as I know, nobody has ever spotted a whale in Weymouth Bay. While it is very unlikely you'll see one in the bay, you might actually spot one out here." She gestured towards the open sea.

"But suppose I *do* find a whale in Weymouth Bay?" Harvey asked. "Would I be super famous?"

"You'd certainly get your name in the local paper," replied Wendy. "I suppose that would make you somewhat famous. But you'd be a hero on this boat if you could find some dolphins for us. By the way, Carter told me he won't be taking us much past the tip of Portland on this trip. We, or I should say *you*, could expand our search area for us by flying further south and having a look around."

"That sounds good to me." Harvey immediately installed a fresh battery in the drone and took off heading south, away from the mainland.

* * *

The drone had been in the air for only a few minutes when Harvey spotted something exciting. "Oh, wow!" he called out. "There's lots of splashing ahead, and a tonne of seagulls, and I think there are cetaceans…boatloads of cetaceans! They're jumping and splashing and swimming really fast!"

"I hope you aren't having us on again," the Tank scowled.

"Are they really dolphins?" Wendy asked eagerly.

"It depends on what you mean by dolphins," Harvey smiled. He couldn't see Wendy's face with the goggles on, but he could imagine her rolling her eyes. "Do you mean toothed whales, or do you mean something like a bottlenose dolphin?"

"Bottlenose, Harvey, of course I mean bottlenose," Wendy groaned.

"Not a hundred percent sure yet. But they *are* porpoising through the water."

"So they're porpoises?"

"It depends what you mean by *porpoise*. Do you mean any creature that porpoises through the water, or a toothed whale that's a cousin to the dolphin?"

"Yes, I mean that kind of porpoise! Like a dolphin, but with a shorter beak." She muttered under her breath, "Note to self, buy your own drone."

Harvey was much closer now and could easily make out the distinctive beak of a dolphin. "No, they aren't porpoises, but they certainly *are* toothed whales." Not wanting to keep the others in suspense any longer, he added, "I'm pretty sure they're bottlenose dolphins, and there are forty or fifty of them."

"Forty of fifty, that's incredible! Simply amazing!" exclaimed the Tank.

A general murmur of excitement rippled throughout the boat, followed by a brief discussion between Wendy and Carter.

"We're going to head further out to sea," Wendy announced, "but this is going to take some extra time. So, instead of heading east to Durdle Door as originally planned, we'll have to head straight back to Weymouth after we count the dolphins."

Several of the volunteers had never seen a dolphin in their lives, so they were all in agreement that the diversion would be worthwhile.

★ ★ ★

A few minutes later, the boat passed the tip of Portland and approached the area where the drone could be seen hovering.

"Look over there!" shouted James, who spotted the creatures first. "Harvey was right. There are lots of them!"

Soon the others could all see them too. There were shouts of "Wow!" and "That's amazing," and the Tank kept saying, "Well I never, well I never," over and over again.

"There are more coming!" Harvey called out excitedly. "There's another pod coming from the south, and this one's even bigger."

Carter slowed the boat down, being careful not to approach the dolphins too closely.

Now all the passengers on the boat could see the dolphins from the first pod without even using the binoculars. Then suddenly, without any warning, the pod changed direction and swam towards the boat. Carter cut the engines as the pod swam around them, jumping and diving and twisting in the air. In less than a minute, the larger, second pod of dolphins arrived, and the *Sidon* was surrounded by what appeared to be hundreds of dolphins. The group watched in awe, while Harvey continued to film from the air.

"Wow, wow, wow! This is truly incredible," the Tank beamed. "One of the best experiences of my life."

And then, as if by command from the dolphin in chief, the dolphins darted off towards the open sea, leaving the volunteer dolphin spotters feeling like they had just been part of something really special.

"I ain't seen nothin' like that before." Carter was leaning against the gunwale, shaking his head and gazing out to sea. "That was truly somethin' that was."

"It certainly was," said Wendy. Then she remembered why they had come. "Oh bother, I completely forgot to count them. Did anyone else remember to count?"

"Don't worry about it," Harvey assured her. "For a small fee, I'll let you have a copy of the video."

"How about you agree to share the footage, and I won't throw you overboard, Harvey Ranger," Wendy teased.

Chuckles could be heard from most of the volunteers.

"Sounds like a good deal," Harvey agreed. "I don't want to miss the next trip on account of my being dead. I'll send you a copy of the video."

The Ginger Santa tapped Harvey on the shoulder. "You be careful, laddie, or that sass of yours is going to get you into a wee bit of trouble one of these days."

Harvey nodded as he flew the drone back to the *Sidon* and Carter turned the boat towards Weymouth Harbour.

After docking, Carter slipped Harvey a fiver and said, "There you go, lad. You saved me a lot more than that in diesel fuel today."

Chapter 7

THE SUSPICIOUS CHARACTER

Mr Ranger walked in the front door around three o'clock in the afternoon. The rest of the family were all gathered around the TV, watching the video footage Harvey had created that morning. Mr Ranger caught the tail end of the video as he walked into the living room.

"Wow, Harvey," said Mr Ranger. "That's impressive. Would you mind starting it over so I can see the whole thing?"

Harvey started the video from the beginning, including the group shot with everybody waving.

"It looks like a good turnout," said Mr Ranger. "But what about Miss Gale? She popped in for some eclairs the other day, and she told me she was looking forward to going on that trip."

"She had a puncture and couldn't make it on time. Another man took her place, so the boat was still filled up. James nicknamed the man the Ginger Santa."

When the video ended, everyone congratulated Harvey on his excellent filmmaking skills and commented on the amazing spectacle of the dolphin mega pod.

"That was incredible, Harvey," said Mrs Ranger. "You certainly wouldn't have been able to capture great video like that without a drone."

"Thanks, Mum. It was absolutely brilliant being able to shoot it with the FPV goggles. It felt like I was really there."

"Miss Gale is going to be very disappointed when she realizes what she missed out on," said Mr Ranger. "Let's take her over some more chocolate eclairs and fix that puncture for her. Why don't you come with me Harvey, and then you can tell her all about it?"

★ ★ ★

Father and son were soon on their bikes, pedalling over to Miss Gale's place. Miss Gale lived alone in a small, well kept, red brick house with two palm trees in the front garden. Mr Ranger walked up the front path and rang the bell. Miss Gale was wearing exercise clothes and was out of breath when she came and opened the door.

Mr Ranger spoke first. "Sorry, Miss Gale. Have we caught you at a bad time?"

"Not a bad time at all," she replied with a slight American accent. "I was just working out on my new fitness trampoline. Does wonders for my bone density and my metabolism. But it's always nice to chat with a fellow artist."

As a young woman, Miss Gale, having obtained a degree in history from Oxford, had moved to Weymouth in the early sixties for the scenic coastline and fresh salty air. Her real name was Gale Falkner. She had, for a short time, been married to Richard Falkner, but he had died some thirty years prior in a boating accident.

Miss Gale spied the box in Mr Ranger's hand. "Would you like to come in for a cup of tea?" she asked.

"Thanks, but we're here to drop off these." Mr Ranger handed her the box of eclairs. "And Harvey told me you missed the boat trip this morning due to a punctured tyre. We were wondering if we could fix it for you?"

"Oh, thank you. You know I think your eclairs are to die for," she said, accepting the box. "I've just finished the ones I bought the other day. It would be wonderful if you could fix my tyre. I've lived alone most of my life and learned to manage most things for myself, but removing those tyres can be quite a struggle."

She led the way around the back of the house and pulled the bike out of the shed. Mr Ranger passed Harvey the tools he had brought with him. "There you go, Harvey," he smiled. "I need to go back to work this afternoon, and it wouldn't do for me to have dirt under my fingernails."

Harvey didn't mind. Fixing punctures was something he had lots of experience with. He quickly removed the wheel from the bicycle and set it on the ground. The cause of the flat tyre was immediately obvious.

"It doesn't look like I can patch this one, Dad. It looks like someone slashed it with a knife." He held up the wheel so they could both see. "We're going to have to replace the tyre *and* the tube."

"Oh deary me," said Miss Gale. "I wonder why someone would do that. The shed was locked, so they must have picked the lock, slashed my tyre, and then locked the shed again. That's very strange indeed."

"It doesn't sound like your typical act of vandalism, does it?" said Mr Ranger. "Picking a lock requires a certain level of expertise."

"Yes, I wonder why someone would want to do that. What would be the benefit? Who would gain anything from doing something so ridiculous?" she said.

"The Ginger Santa would," said Harvey.

They both turned and looked at him in surprise.

"The Ginger Santa. He's the man from the boat this morning. He took your spot when you didn't show up. He's a tall man with ginger hair and a bushy beard. That's why we call him the Ginger Santa."

"Oh good gracious," said Miss Gale. "I think you might be right. You know Mrs Murphy, who lives on the corner? Well she's a bit on the nosy side and pays a little too much attention to other people's business. When she was walking her dog this morning, I was out pulling some weeds. She told me that she'd seen a suspicious-looking character in the neighbourhood with ginger hair and a long beard. It all makes sense now. It seems like he came here and slashed my tyre so I would miss the boat. Then he took my spot."

"Yes, but how did he know you were going on the trip?" Harvey questioned. "He must have found out somehow."

"I've no idea. It's all very peculiar."

"You should call the police," said Mr Ranger. "Harvey shot some video today. It includes a group shot with the Ginger Santa in it. I'm sure he would be happy to share it with you and the police."

"That would be great. Thank you, Harvey," said Miss Gale.

"You're welcome." Harvey looked down at the slashed tube that was still in his hand. "Dad, what are we going to do about this?"

"Don't you worry about this, Miss Gale," said Mr Ranger. "We'll head down to Nick's Bike Fix and buy a new tyre and tube, then we'll come right back and fix your wheel. You'll be back in the saddle before tea time."

Chapter 8

MUM'S THE WORD

On arrival back at the Ranger residence, Harvey re-played the segment of the video from that morning that included the group shot. The camera stayed on the group for a full six seconds, and during that entire time the Ginger Santa was scratching his nose. *Either he has a very itchy nose,* Harvey thought, *or he's doing that deliberately to cover his face.* He decided to send the video to Miss Gale anyway. She would enjoy seeing the dolphins, and there might be something there that the police could work with.

Harvey went down to the living room where his mum and dad were chatting. "Look what your father worked on today," said Mrs Ranger, holding up a water-colour painting showing four white ducks in front of a small thatched-roof cottage. "It's from Moles Dash Farm. What do you think?"

"It looks to me like someone tried to paint a picture of a farm when a photograph would have looked a lot better and taken less time."

"Well, I think it's lovely!" said Mrs Ranger. "He's done a super job on the ducks. He's never painted ducks before."

Harvey looked more closely. "Yes, those ducks are some of the best painted ducks I have seen since breakfast. They're much better than the great white amoeba he painted last time, the one that was supposed to be sheep."

"You wouldn't appreciate a painting of ducks and a cottage even if Monet painted it."

"That's because if Monet had just painted this picture, then he would still be alive, and no one appreciates great art until the artist is dead. So, basically, I'm normal."

"Normal? That's a bit of a stretch, Harvey. But we love you just the way you are."

"I'm going to update my will," Mr Ranger grinned. "I want to make sure Jack and Sally will get rich selling my paintings after I die."

"And I'm going to hang this painting in the hall by the front door," said Mrs Ranger.

She went into the hall and proceeded to take down another picture of an old man ploughing. She hung the new picture in its place. "That's a great spot for it," she declared, just as Harvey joined her in the hall.

"It's certainly a lot better than the one you took down. That old painting has been hanging there literally forever, and I never really liked it. It looks like a man ploughing a field with a bicycle, and that makes no sense. The Duck Dash painting is way better."

"It's not supposed to be a bicycle," corrected Mrs Ranger. "It's some kind of old fashioned plough that was pulled by horses. And it's Moles Dash, not Duck Dash."

"Same thing," Harvey shrugged.

"No, Harvey. They are not the same thing. Moles are moles and ducks are ducks. About the only similarity is that they both eat worms."

"That reminds me," Harvey said. "I'm feeling a bit peckish. Like a duck."

"We're having homemade pizza tonight," said Mrs Ranger. "If you want something to hold you over, there are some sausage rolls in Dad's backpack by the front door. He brought them home with him earlier this afternoon."

The backpack was still on the floor in the hall, right at Harvey's feet. He bent over and unzipped it. Inside was one of the familiar boxes from Auntie Bunny's. As he pulled the box out, his dad's Swiss Army knife slid off the top of the box and into the bottom of the backpack. He grabbed the knife and used it to cut the piece of tape that held the box shut. With the box lid open, he straightened up and looked at his mum.

"How many sausage rolls can I have?"

"Just take one, or you won't want your tea. You need to make sure there's one left over for both Sally and Jack."

Harvey took the box into the kitchen and set it down on the counter. If he ate the sausage roll over the sink, he wouldn't have to use a plate. Not making a plate dirty meant he wouldn't have to *wash* a plate and that, he convinced himself, was better for the environment.

Mr Ranger walked past Harvey and went to the window. "It's cooled off quite a bit, hasn't it?" he observed as he closed the window.

Harvey didn't reply. There was something about the way his dad walked that triggered a connection in his brain. Harvey knew that each person walked in a unique way, much like each person has a unique fingerprint. He'd read a spy novel in which the main character would place a small stone in his shoe so he wouldn't be recognised by his gait.

While mulling over the connection Harvey continued to finish his sausage roll and then absentmindedly started a second and a third. He was just finishing the last one when it clicked. His dad walked like the Ginger Santa.

He pondered that connection for a moment. How could his dad possibly be the Ginger Santa? He had been off painting that morning, but he *had* been away long enough to go on the trip and paint Moles Dash Farm. He'd also found his dad's Swiss Army knife in his backpack, so his dad had the means to slash a tire. But why would his dad be dressing up like a Scottish Santa Claus and going on dolphin watching trips? That made no sense. He decided to have another look in the backpack for more clues.

Leaving the empty box on the table, he returned to the front hall. His mum and dad were chatting in the living room again as he peeked into his dad's backpack. The knife was still there, sitting on top of a black tee shirt. He lifted the black tee shirt up and there, on the bottom of the backpack, was a mass of ginger hair. He pulled the curly mass out of the backpack and held it up. Attached to the hair was a silicone face mask. The mask was the face of the Ginger Santa. Harvey's mind was reeling. There was only one way to make any sense of it: he would have to confront his dad.

Harvey walked into the living room, carrying the mask. His mum and dad looked up as he entered. They both smiled at him.

"What have you got there, Harvey?" asked Mr Ranger. "Are you getting ready for Halloween?"

"No, I found this in your backpack," replied Harvey. And then he decided to just come right out with it. "Are you the Ginger Santa?" he asked.

Mr Ranger smiled even more. "So proud of you, son. You figured it out."

"Figured out what? That you like spotting dolphins so much you would dress up like a Scottish Santa Claus and slash an old lady's bicycle tyre?"

"Well, sort of, but that's not the whole story. Have a seat." He gestured to the chair across from him and Harvey sat down in it. "You see, there is a little family secret that you don't know about yet. Are you ready for it?"

"I'm all ears," said Harvey. He wouldn't normally say "I'm all ears," but he had recently read it in a book and it just seemed like the right thing to say.

His father continued. "So you know how I worked for the Ministry of Defence, which we usually just refer to as the MOD? Well, it's true that I worked for the MOD, but I worked for a very special department within the MOD called MI5."

"You were a spy?" said Harvey in surprise.

"No, not a spy," replied Mr Ranger. He turned and looked at his wife. "Can you imagine me being a spy?"

Mrs Ranger smiled. "I'm sure you would make a wonderful spy," she said.

"So what were you then, if you weren't a spy?" asked Harvey.

"I was a counterspy."

Harvey was about to deliver one of his annoying "same thing" comments but decided that the matter being discussed was a bit too serious for clowning around.

"A counterspy," continued Mr Ranger, "is kind of like the opposite of a spy. They're spy catchers."

"So you *were* a spy catcher. What are you now?"

"I'm still a spy catcher. When I retired from MI5 to become a baker, I wasn't completely happy. Don't get me wrong. I love running Auntie Bunny's, but I missed some of the work at MI5. Fortunately for me, I possess a rather unique set of skills and Box 500, as we like to call MI5 within government circles, needs me for special projects from time to time. The best part now is that I get to do all the fun stuff and other people do most of the paperwork for me. It's the best of both worlds."

"What about all the paintings?" asked Harvey. "Does someone from Box 500 paint those for you?"

"No, those are my handiwork. Being a painter is just a cover story for my other work. When I go away I actually create those paintings myself. Like you, art wasn't really my thing, but over the years I've really grown to enjoy painting. Some of them aren't too bad, are they?"

"No, they're not. The ones you've been bringing home lately look like you actually know what you're doing. But hang on. Did Box 500 hire you to slash Miss Gale's tyre so you could go dolphin spotting?"

"No, not dolphin spotting. I was tank spotting."

"Tanks! There weren't any...oh, you mean the Tank! You were watching that stocky man on the boat."

"Exactly. You catch on quickly, Harvey. By the way, you and James should be a little more discreet when you give someone a nickname."

"So is the Tank a spy?"

"We're not exactly sure what he is, but we know for sure that he is associated with an international crime syndicate, and we think they're up to something."

"Were you able to learn anything about him today, or figure out what he's up to?"

"I'm not able to discuss that with you, Harvey. That's top secret. But did you observe anything?"

"I think it would be very hard to knock him over," said Harvey. "And he was nearly deaf in his left ear."

"So you heard him say that. But do you know why he was nearly deaf in his left ear?"

"No. I missed that bit."

"It's because he's a bagpiper."

"So how did you figure out he was a piper?"

"I just asked him why he had trouble hearing with his left ear, and he told me that he'd played the bagpipes for years and that it was a common problem amongst pipers."

Harvey was disappointed. "So you're not exactly Sherlock Holmes," he said.

"No, sorry. Only Sherlock Holmes is as good as Sherlock Holmes. Did you observe anything else about the Tank?"

"He seemed genuinely interested in cetaceans."

"I think you're right about that. Did you see how excited he got when you spotted the dolphins?"

"My eyes were covered with my goggles, but I could hear him. By the way, you interrupted me when I was introducing myself. Was that intentional?"

"Yes, it was. I knew you were going to be shooting a video that would likely include the Tank, so I thought it better that he didn't know your full name. The less these people know about you the better."

"But what about poor Miss Gale? You slashed her tyre and she didn't get to come on the trip."

"Technically speaking, it wasn't her tyre. About five years ago, Mum encouraged her to try biking instead of driving around Weymouth. We had an extra bike in the shed and so we said she could use it until she figured out if cycling was going to work out for her. She offered to return it, but we said she could just keep using it until we needed it back. We haven't needed it back, and she still uses the bike."

"She must have been disappointed to miss the trip."

"Yes, I feel bad about that," said Mr Ranger. "I'm not sure the eclairs completely made it up to her, but if she knew the whole story I'm sure she would be okay with it."

"You still broke into her shed," said Harvey.

"It would appear that way, wouldn't it?" agreed Mr Ranger. "I can't explain that one to you at the moment. You're just going to have to trust me on that one and believe me when I say that I didn't break any laws or do anything I shouldn't have done. Do you see now why I needed to go on the boat ride?"

"Yes, I do. So who else knows about Box 500?"

"Mum and Jack know. Sally doesn't. Outside of those people, I'm not authorised to tell you who does and doesn't know. I need to be able to trust you to keep quiet about this. Mum and I decided you would be ready to tell when you were able to pass a test. You passed the test today when you figured out I was the Ginger Santa."

"You did well today," Mrs Ranger chimed in. "Jack was twelve before he figured it out."

"Oh, I can't wait to tell Jack I figured it out before him."

"Harvey, mum's the word on this one. Remember that loose lips sink ships. After you leave this room, you can't talk about this again except in extenuating circumstances," cautioned Mr Ranger.

"Sorry," said Harvey. "Mum's the word."

Chapter 9

THE HURRICANE

Harvey had mixed feelings about his father being a counterspy. On the one hand, he was proud of his dad. On the other hand, he was frustrated that he couldn't tell his friends about it or even discuss it with Jack. Nevertheless, he walked around with his head held just a little bit higher, not just proud of his dad but also pleased with himself for figuring out that his dad was the Ginger Santa.

During the weeks following the discovery, Harvey split his free time between searching for whales with his drones and researching MI5 on his laptop. There were no whales to be seen, but information on the counterspy agency was readily available on the internet. He learned that the *MI* stood for Military Intelligence and that number five was a department number. There had been an MI 1, 2, 3 and 4 at some point in the past, but there was no evidence that these existed today. It seemed that only MI5 and MI6 were still around. Harvey also learned that MI5 was referred to as Box 500 after its wartime address of PO Box 500 in London.

★ ★ ★

The regular routine of life continued for Harvey until one Thursday morning in mid-October, when his personal electronic assistant woke him up with a reminder that the day was going to be a little bit different.

"Good morning Harvey, it's oh-six-hundred hours," Alexa announced. "It's currently ten degrees centigrade and overcast. Light showers are expected this morning. You have a school trip today. You need to be at school for oh-seven-hundred hours."

Now this was no ordinary school trip to somewhere like a nature centre, where the class might make observations about the plants and animals they observed. No, this was the school trip that the older students always said was *the best trip ever.* This was the day of the long-awaited trip to the Tower of London, where there were actual dungeons and priceless crown jewels, a place where kings and queens had lived and died.

Miss Loveday, Harvey's teacher, had made it clear that the coach would be leaving the school at precisely seven in the morning. "We won't wait for anybody," she had warned. "If you aren't there when the coach leaves, then we leave without you. There will be absolutely no exceptions."

He knew being late was simply not an option, so Harvey climbed out of bed quickly. He was surprised to see that Jack's bed was empty and had already been neatly made.

After making his own bed, Harvey followed his nose downstairs and into the kitchen where Mr Ranger had whipped up a batch of banana and chocolate chip muffins.

"Morning, Harvey. Try to limit yourself to four muffins, please. You need to save some for the rest of the family. But eat this first." He passed Harvey a plate with three eggs, three sausages, baked beans, and fried tomatoes. "Sorry, you're eating by yourself today. I've already had my breakfast. Mum and Sally haven't come down yet and Jack's gone to Jasper."

"Anyone that gets up that early for a rocks and minerals club must have rocks in their head," Harvey scoffed as he devoured the first sausage.

He had polished off the third sausage and was working on the eggs when he heard the sound of heavy rain.

"The forecast was for light showers," he said. "That sounds like a torrential downpour."

"Not everything is as it seems," said Mr Ranger. "Sometimes there are alternate explanations for the things we observe."

An alternate explanation for heavy rain? Harvey listened again, but the sound stopped almost immediately for just a second and then restarted. "That's weird," Harvey said. "Rain doesn't normally do that. What's going on?"

As if in answer to his question, Sally bounced noisily into the kitchen. Like her mother, Sally was outgoing and bubbly, but she'd also inherited a passion for adventure from her father's side of the family. The bubbliness and adventure came together like two air masses forming a tornado, and on many days it seemed to the other family members that a tornado had in fact swept through the house.

Harvey noticed that Sally was carrying a rain stick made from a wrapping paper tube and, from the sound of it, filled with rice. Waving the rain stick around, Sally began improvising a dance that looked like a cross between the Nutcracker and someone rowing a boat in a hurricane. From her mouth came a discordant sound best described as a wild cat doing a Gregorian chant. Harvey and Mr Ranger just watched for a moment, both recognising that the entertainment value far exceeded their need for peace and quiet.

The noise was so intense that Harvey, with his back to the door, didn't hear his mother come downstairs and into the kitchen. He was startled when he suddenly heard her voice beside him.

"Sally, sit down!" she called out above the din. Sally rowed herself over to her seat and flopped into her chair.

"Are you all set for your trip today, Harvey?" Mrs Ranger asked.

"I'm probably gonna need some extra money for food."

"Haven't we already paid the school to provide you with lunch?"

"Yes. But there are no seconds with packed lunches, and the lunch ladies pack the same for me as they do for Molly Pinker."

Molly Pinker had petite parents and was an August baby, making her the youngest and, by far, the smallest member of Harvey's class. Harvey, on the other hand, was born on September 1st, only minutes after the August 31st cut-off for the academic year. This made him the oldest and, by virtue of his genes, the tallest student in the class. Consequently, Mrs Ranger wasn't unsympathetic to Harvey's situation.

"Why don't you take an extra sandwich? Remember, money doesn't grow on trees," she said.

"Technically speaking, mother, money does grow on trees since money is made from paper and paper comes from trees."

Mrs Ranger rolled her eyes.

With a final bite of sausage, Harvey excused himself from the table and started to make a cheese and Marmite sandwich. Sally watched in mock horror as Harvey spread a thin layer of Marmite on the bread.

"That stuff's disgusting," she teased. "Only someone with no taste buds could eat that stuff."

Harvey was well aware of the love-hate relationship most people seemed to have with Marmite.

"Sally, there are two types of people in the world: people who love Marmite, and people who spread it too thick," countered Harvey.

"No," she retorted. "There are two types of people in this world. Normal people and you."

They gave each other the stink eye as Harvey grabbed his backpack and shoved the sandwich inside.

"Bye Mum, bye Dad," he said, dodging his mother's attempt to kiss him on the cheek. Sally flung herself at him with one of her signature hug-tackles that she liked to call a *hackle*

While these were somewhat painful, you knew you were in Sally's good books if she gave you a hackle.

"Ummph!" Harvey groaned as his solar plexus absorbed the brunt of the somewhat more aggressive than normal hackle. "Love you, Sal," he grinned, as he turned and walked out the door.

Chapter 10

COACH CLASS TO LONDON

Alexa was right about the light showers. The pitter-patter of the first drops of rain could be heard on the roof of the bike shed as Harvey locked his bike. Slinging his backpack over his shoulder, he pulled the hood of his coat over his head and ran across the car park towards the coach that would be taking them to London. Beside the coach, Miss Summer Loveday was standing, wearing a yellow raincoat and holding a clipboard precariously between her knees while she tried to open her bright red umbrella.

"Mornin', Miss Loveday," Harvey said. "Miserable weather, isn't it?"

"Good morning, Harvey. I don't think it's miserable weather. The fresh earthy smell, when it starts to rain, is simply divine. It's all about your perspective." She closed her eyes and inhaled a deep breath of fresh air before continuing. "Oh, I just remembered that you're the designated photographer for the day. Did you bring your camera, Harvey?"

"Yes, Miss. I brought my camera. Actually, I brought two with me," Harvey replied before climbing the steps into the coach. As the photographer, he liked to sit in the first row so he could take pictures out the front window. The front seat on the left was still available, so he placed his backpack on the floor and sat down. A moment later, James arrived and sat next to him. Before long, all the other students were in their seats.

Miss Loveday climbed on the coach to do a final headcount. All nineteen students of Class 6B were accounted for, but the headmaster, who was supposed to come on the trip, was missing.

"If Mr Hawking is off time, shouldn't we leave without him?" Harvey questioned.

"Off time, Harvey? Does that mean *late*?"

"Yes, Miss. It's the opposite of on time. It's logical, isn't it?"

"I suppose so, but late or off time or whatever you want to call it, we can't leave without Mr Hawking."

"But you said the coach wouldn't wait for anyone."

"I did, but Mr Hawking isn't just anyone. He's an adult as well as being the Headmaster. The Tower of London requires one adult for every ten students, and since there are nineteen of you, we need two adults. Mr Hawking volunteers to come on this trip every year."

"There aren't nineteen of me, Miss. There is just one of me," Harvey quipped. "Well, it's a very good thing there's only one of you," his teacher smirked.

Harvey pondered the merits of spending three and a half hours on a coach with eighteen other versions of himself. The other Harveys would likely drive him bonkers. Miss Loveday was probably right.

Harvey's thoughts were interrupted by Miss Loveday announcing to the class that she was going into the school to use the phone to call Mr Hawking. "Unfortunately," she said, "I dropped my mobile this morning and it's not working anymore."

"I've got a phone built into my camera, Miss," said Harvey. "You can use it to call Mr Hawking."

"Don't you mean the camera is built into your phone, Harvey?"

"I suppose you could put it that way. But it's all about your perspective, Miss," he replied with a cheeky grin.

Miss Loveday rolled her eyes. "Harvey, would you mind if I borrowed your camera to call Mr Hawking?"

Harvey unlocked his camera and passed it to Miss Loveday.

"This looks just like a regular mobile phone to me, Harvey," she commented before calling the headmaster. She chatted with the headmaster for a minute and then passed the phone back to Harvey. "His car wouldn't start, so he decided to walk. He'll be a few more minutes. "She looked quizzically at Harvey. "I'm curious," she asked. "What's your other camera?"

"It's a drone."

"I should have guessed. Well, you might as well make use of it." She stood up and turned to the back of the coach. "Alright, people. Everybody off. The rain has stopped, and we're going to do a dronie group shot while we wait for Mr Hawking."

The class lined up in two rows in front of the coach. Harvey used his phone to control the drone, and when it was at a suitable height above and in front of the group he hollered, "Okay everybody, say...Mr Hawking's coming!" He had meant to say "say cheese," but his eye had been drawn to some motion at the top of the screen, and he'd realised that the headmaster was in fact walking up the drive.

The class all repeated, "Mr Hawking's coming!" which resulted in a lot of well-timed giggles and smiles. Harvey quickly snapped the photo and landed the drone.

"Chop-chop Harvey," Miss Loveday urged. "Get your cameras packed away. Mr Hawking's not going to be happy if he sees those." Harvey folded the arms of the drone and stowed it back in its case. The case was back in the backpack, and the zipper was just being zipped shut as Mr Hawking walked up to the group.

Mr Hawking was a big man with vocal cords to match. It didn't help that he was nearly deaf in one ear. "Ranger!" he boomed. "What was that infernal flying machine I just saw buzzing about above the coach?"

"Just a flying camera sir," Harvey responded sheepishly. "Miss Loveday made me the official photographer for the day."

"Well, I certainly hope you have another camera, because you aren't bringing that thing on this trip. Take it into the school and put it in your locker." He turned to the rest of the class. "Alright then, everyone back on the coach. What are you waiting for?"

Harvey, thankful that Mr Hawking hadn't asked for details about his other camera, made a quick dash into the school to stash the drone in his locker.

"You're lucky he didn't confiscate it," James whispered as Harvey returned to his seat.

"I suppose he didn't want to run into the school himself," replied Harvey. "He was probably tired from the walk."

Harvey discreetly checked Google Maps on his phone as the coach pulled out of Mulberry Lane. "Three hours and twenty-two minutes to go," he told his friend. "It's going to be a long trip. Good thing there's a loo at the back."

Miss Loveday was well aware that three hours and twenty-two minutes was a lot of time, and she had come prepared. She picked up the microphone for the coach's PA system and turned it on with a crackle. "To your right," she said, pointing out the window, "is the River Wey." She went on to explain the significance of the river and its role in the growth of the area. She pointed out that the River Wey came up out of the ground in the village of Upwey, that it broadened in Broadwey, and that the mouth of the river was in Weymouth. *Predictable,* thought Harvey, *just the way life should be.*

The remainder of the trip was spent going through the regular part of the school day as best Miss Loveday was able to make that happen on a coach. For an added bonus, she threw in a colouring contest of the crown jewels. It had been a long time since Harvey had coloured with crayons and, like several of his classmates, he was surprised at how satisfying the experience was.

Chapter 11

TWO SLICES OF PICKLE AND A BEEFEATER

Geography, history, and maths lessons had been completed before the coach stopped near the Tower of London shortly before eleven. Miss Loveday reminded the class about staying with their assigned buddy.

The door hissed with escaping air as the students rose from their seats, shuffled towards the front of the coach, and climbed down the two steps onto the pavement.

Their guide was waiting for them. He was wearing a large hat, a navy blue tunic with red stripes, and navy blue trousers. He had a friendly face, a grey beard, and an infectious smile that made Harvey think he was about to share a funny joke.

Weybourne College Class 6B all gathered round to hear what their guide had to say.

"Come closer, young ones. I don't mind raising my voice, but I don't want to shout my head off. There have been too many heads coming off around here over the past thousand years. We don't need any more of that."

The students laughed and moved closer.

"That's it, get close enough so you can see the hair up my nose."

The class moved closer still. *Poor Molly,* thought Harvey. *She always has to stand at the front of the group and get spat on.*

"That's better," the guide said. "Welcome to Her Majesty's Palace and Fortress, the Tower of London. Today, I am going to be giving you a tour of the Tower. I am not a tour guide; I am a Yeoman Warder. That means it's my job to protect the Tower and the crown jewels. But, I also give tours–as some of the more astute amongst you may have already gathered. Any questions so far?"

"Are you a Beefeater?" asked Ryan Jenkins.

"That's correct, I am a Beefeater. And yes, I do love a nice roast beef sandwich with two slices of pickle and just a hint of Marmite. No tomatoes please, I'm allergic to tomatoes. But 'Beefeater' is just a nickname and has nothing to do with my culinary preferences. Nobody knows for sure where the name comes from. *I* have a nickname, too. My real name is Nicholas Sparks, but you can call me Yeoman Nick."

He took a breath and looked around the group. "Now, let's see how clever you are. What do you see behind me?"

"The Tower of London," the class responded in unison.

"No, you're all wrong," said the yeoman. "Behind me is something called grass. I'm surprised you aren't familiar with it. Behind the *grass* is the Tower of London."

The students laughed again.

"Did you know that parts of the Tower of London are nearly a thousand years old? The White Tower, which is the main one, was built by William the Conqueror in 1078." Yeoman Nick paused and looked up. "And what do you see above me?" he asked, looking up into the sky.

"The sky," replied the class.

"Wrong again," said the yeoman. "Above me is my hat. As you can see, my hat is quite tall and my head doesn't go all the way inside." He took the hat off, revealing his thick, tousled grey hair.

Harvey, who was discreetly holding his camera phone, snapped a photo.

"Take a look in there," Yeoman Nick said and turned the hat over so the class could see how much space was inside. "The reason I wear a tall hat like that is that it makes me look bigger and more intimidating. If I look bigger and more intimidating, you're more likely to pay attention and less likely to try and pinch the Crown Jewels." He looked menacingly around at the group. "I hope that none of you are thinking that pinching the crown jewels is a good idea. Now follow me."

Chapter 12

TALES FROM THE TOWERS

Yeoman Nick turned and led the group across a walkway over a wide moat and into an arched entryway between two cylindrical towers. "We are walking through the Byward Tower. If you look up, you will see a large drop gate. This drop gate is called a portcullis. It was built in the thirteenth century and weighs over fifteen hundred kilograms. No one knows how old the rope is, so you'd better walk quickly under it. There are ten nasty spikey bits at the bottom. If that thing came down on you, you would bear a striking resemblance to a large Swiss cheese covered in ketchup."

"I like him. I think he's funny," Harvey said, as he took a few quick steps under the portcullis. Yeoman Nick was most likely joking about the age of the rope, but it was best to play it safe.

"Yeah," James agreed. "I think we're going to enjoy this."

The yeoman stopped with his back against a wall and beckoned the students to draw closer. "Behind me," he said, "is the Bell Tower. But we're going to save that for later. What I want to talk to you about now is Mint Street." He gestured up the street to his right and then turned to look at Harvey. "Why do you think it's called Mint Street, lad?"

Before Harvey had a chance to answer, Ryan Jenkins yelled out, "Because it tastes minty!"

"Ahh, the class clown has revealed himself," said Yeoman Nick. "Maybe you could test your theory for us and give the paving stones a good lick, or does someone have a better answer for me?"

"Did they make money here?" Harvey offered.

"That is correct. We are talking about the word 'mint' that comes from the Latin word 'moneta' and not the word 'mint' that is normally prefaced with 'pepper'. So, why do you think the king would want his coinage produced within these walls?"

"To stop people from stealing the money," replied Harvey.

"That is also correct, and whoever controlled the Tower controlled the money. And being in control of the money meant you got to slap your face on the coins. No doubt having your subjects walk around with pictures of you in their pockets was a good reminder to them of who was in charge."

Yeoman Nick pointed towards the building across the street. "The Royal Mint was located inside the Tower of London for over five hundred years, and for most of that time it was located in that building on the left." He paused. "I'm sure you have all heard of Sir Isaac Newton. Who can tell me what he's famous for?"

"He figured out that what goes up must come down," responded James.

"That's one way of putting it. Newton said that an object will remain in motion unless acted upon by something else. In your example, an object would just keep going up and up if it wasn't acted upon by gravity," the yeoman explained. "We call that Newton's First Law. Newton came up with two other laws for a total of three laws. Newton's three laws are called 'Newton's Three Laws'. There must have been some very sharp minds working overtime to come up with that name."

Next, Yeoman Nick pointed up to the second floor. "Here's a little known fact for you. Sir Isaac Newton was the Master of the Mint for 27 years, and there, behind those windows, was his study. Newton took his job as

Master of the Mint very seriously. So seriously, in fact, that he would disguise himself as a regular citizen and go into bars and taverns to gather evidence against counterfeiters. He chased one coiner for three years before finally catching him. It didn't end well for that man, as you might well imagine. Let's just say that when he died, he would have preferred that Newton's First Law didn't exist."

He paused for a breath. "Now follow me down Water Lane, and we'll learn all about why it's not a good idea to try and blow up the Palace of Westminster with the king inside."

He stopped a short distance down a cobbled street with his back to a four-storey building. "Any questions so far?"

Harvey raised his hand. "So there's a Middle Tower, a Byward Tower, a Bell Tower, and a White Tower. How many towers are there altogether?"

"There are twenty-one in total," replied Yeoman Nick. "There used to be twenty-two, but the Lion Tower was knocked down in the 1800s."

"So how come it's just called the Tower of London and not the *Towers* of London?"

"I'm impressed," responded Yeoman Nick. "This class doesn't just have a clown. It has a lawyer, too.

Young man, I don't have an answer to that question, but I assure you I will take it up with Her Majesty the Queen the next time I see her."

Harvey could tell by the look on the yeoman's face that a meeting with the queen was unlikely, but he decided that from then on he would refer to it as the *Towers* of London, for the sake of accuracy.

No one else had any questions, so Yeoman Nick continued to tell them all about Guy Fawkes and how he, and some co-conspirators, attempted to blow up the parliament buildings on November fifth, 1605. "The king was not at all happy about the prospect of being blown to bits so he had Guy Fawkes brought to Queen's House behind me to be questioned." He went on to explain how Guy Fawkes was tortured and eventually confessed, and how he and most of his co-conspirators were brought to justice.

"Now come this way," he instructed. "We're going to learn about a couple of boys who lived here and *didn't* die a bloody death." He led the class further down Water Lane and stopped with his back to a low archway in the outer wall. There was an iron gate in the arch, and through the gate, you could see the Thames River. Water filled the area around the bottom of the gate, and above it, there was a sign that read *Traitors' Gate*.

Yeoman Nick pointed to a tower opposite Traitors' Gate and said, "And here we have the Garden Tower, later renamed the Bloody Tower. I'm not sure why *this* tower was chosen to be called the Bloody Tower. Pretty much all the towers should have been called the Bloody Tower, or they should have called the whole place the Bloody Tower of London."

"Towers," corrected Harvey.

"Thank you, counsellor," said Yeoman Nick. "When I meet with Her Majesty, I will propose we rename it the Bloody Towers of London, and I'll be sure to give you some of the credit."

There was some chuckling before he continued.

"Who has heard the story of the princes in the tower?"

A dozen hands went up.

"So who can tell me what happened to the two princes?"

James piped up. "They were locked in a tower, so they tied bed sheets together and hung them out the window. But they didn't actually escape that way."

The class turned to James, listening.

"When the guards entered their room, the boys were hiding behind their beds. The guards saw the sheets and assumed they had already escaped. When the guards left to chase after them, they left the door open, and the boys escaped through the open door."

The Yeoman smiled. "It sounds like you've been reading Biff and Chip books. The story that happened here is somewhat different. In this story, the boy's father, who was king, died in the year 1483 of natural causes, leaving his twelve-year-old son Edward the Fifth to be the King of England. As a twelve-year-old, the young king didn't even have his driver's licence yet, so it was his Uncle Richard's responsibility to manage things until Edward was old enough. For their own safety, Uncle Richard brought his nephews, Edward and his nine-year-old brother Richard the Duke of York, to the Bloody Towers of London, where they stayed in the Garden Tower in those rooms up there." He gestured to some windows high up in the wall. "Sadly, neither of the boys ever became king. After June 1483, they were never seen again."

"What happened to them?" Molly Pinker piped in.

"Most people think that their mean Uncle Richard had them killed. Others believe he wasn't that mean at all and that the boys were killed by the king who came after him."

From the back of the crowd came the booming voice of Mr Hawking. "There's a third theory," he said, "and it's closer to the Biff and Chip version. Many people believe the younger prince was able to escape the tower before fleeing to Belgium."

"Yes, that is a theory," agreed the Yeoman. "But it's not a very popular one, and I personally consider it to be pretty unlikely." With that, he abruptly turned around and told them the history of Traitors' Gate, then continued to regale the students with stories of murder and mayhem, love and betrayal, ravens and polar bears, as the tour continued on from the Bloody Tower.

They explored the dungeons and many other towers, all with fascinating histories of the people that had at one time lived, worked or died there. Harvey snapped as many pictures as he could without attracting the attention of Mr Hawking. Finally, they stopped to eat lunch in the Cradle Tower Lunchroom.

Chapter 13

THE CROWN JEWELS

After lunch, it was time to see the Crown Jewels. Yeoman Nick led them to the Waterloo Block, where the Crown Jewels were kept. "And now, ladies and gentlemen," he said, "we have come to the highlight of the tour. Inside this building are the Crown Jewels. They are absolutely priceless."

"I always thought the Crown Jewels were worth a lot of money," said Harvey. "But you said they were priceless. Doesn't that mean they're not worth much?"

"Our young lawyer friend here has pointed out a common misunderstanding with regards to the word *priceless*. I didn't say the jewels are priced less or valueless. *Priceless* simply means they are so valuable, a price can't be determined."

"But how much are they worth?" asked Ryan Jenkins.

"Some experts estimate the value of the entire collection at three to five billion pounds. But don't you worry. They're kept safe behind fifteen-centimetre-thick steel doors and bomb-proof glass. In addition to thirty-seven other strapping young yeomen like myself." The yeoman pushed out his chest and flexed his muscles. "There are twenty-two soldiers whose duty it is to protect those jewels."

"Has anyone tried to steal them?" James asked.

"There was an attempt in 1671. A man called Thomas Blood pretended to be a parson and made friends with the keeper of the jewels, whose name was Talbot Edward. Thomas eventually suggested that his nephew, who wasn't *actually* his nephew, marry the daughter of Talbot. When Thomas brought his nephew to meet Talbot, he convinced him to show the jewels to himself, his nephew and a couple of friends. When Talbot showed them the jewels, Thomas bopped him on the head, tied him up and gagged him. They stole the Crown Jewels with Thomas concealing St. Edward's Crown beneath the parson's cloak he was wearing. Fortunately, they were caught before they could leave the outer walls of the Tower. Unfortunately, some of the stolen items were damaged. St Edward's Crown had been flattened with a large wooden mallet, so Thomas could fit it under his cloak. Now please follow me, and we'll go and see the jewels."

Yeoman Nick led the way into the Waterloo Block where the jewels were located. He led the class through the thick steel doors and into the Jewel House. They saw six crowns, including the actual crown Thomas Blood had nearly stolen. They saw many valuable plates, orbs and sceptres, and a spoon that was over eight hundred years old. And they saw many precious diamonds, including the Star of Africa, the largest cut diamond in the world.

Chapter 14

LUKEWARM

With the tour finally over, Yeoman Nick handed out a booklet with a summary of all the history they had learned that day. After thanking him, the class walked back across the moat to the exit.

"Now listen up, everybody," Miss Loveday called. "You can either come into the gift shop with me, or you can wait there near Mr Hawking." She pointed to where Mr Hawking was standing by a large tree to the right of the gift shop.

Most of the class went into the gift shop, but a man standing outside the gift shop selling hot dogs caught James' eye.

"I'm ravenous. Let's get a hot dog from that guy," he said.

"Sounds good to me," Harvey agreed. "I've eaten all my lunch, including my extra Marmite sandwich. It's amazing how just standing around listening uses so much energy."

The man running the cart had shoulder-length brown hair, an arched nose and a prominent chin. He didn't seem to pay much attention to the boys as he served them their hot dogs. They even had to remind him to give them their change.

"That was a bit odd," James said. "He didn't seem to notice us."

"Yeah, he was a strange bloke. He reminded me of the pictures we just saw of Richard the Third. And did you notice he had two different coloured eyes?" He took a bite of his hot dog, "This ain't no *hot* dog, it's more like a lukewarm dog."

"Mine too," said James. "I would go back and complain about it, but something about the way that guy is acting kinda creeps me out."

Both boys turned to take another look at the man and saw Mr Hawking walk up to him and start engaging in a friendly chat. With Mr Hawking distracted, Harvey pulled out his phone and took one last selfie of James and himself with their hot dogs.

Finally, after the hot dogs were eaten and gifts had been purchased, the coach arrived, and the members of Weybourne College, Class 6B climbed aboard and sat down in their seats for the long drive home.

Chapter 15

KING HEROD

Harvey watched out the window as the coach headed west along the M4 past Heathrow Airport. The skies were clear, and he was attempting to count the aeroplanes in the sky when his thoughts were interrupted by Miss Loveday's voice over the PA system.

"I hope everyone enjoyed the tour today. Now that you've all had a little rest, I was wondering if anyone has any questions that they haven't had a chance to ask yet."

Connie Chen raised her hand. "Yeoman Nick said that the man who tried to steal the Crown Jewels was dressed as a parson. What's a parson?"

"A parson," said Miss Loveday, "is a lot like a vicar or a reverend, like Reverend Glennie, our school chaplain. You don't hear the word very often. Has anyone heard of Parson Brown?"

No hands went up. And then, for some reason not immediately apparent, Miss Loveday started singing "Winter Wonderland". The students all thought she might have gone a little bit mad, until she got to the part, "In the meadow, we can build a snowman. Then pretend that he is Parson Brown," at which point there were murmurs of "Ahh" and "I remember now." After that, several students started to join in, and by the time they got to "Later on, we'll conspire, as we dream by the fire," almost everyone on the coach, including the driver, was singing along. The only person not singing was Mr Hawking.

Several boisterous renditions of Winter Wonderland had been belted out before Miss Loveday spoke into the mic once again. "Well done, class. That was wonderful singing and the perfect segue into our next activity. As we do every year at Weybourne College, we're going to be putting on a traditional Christmas play and concert. I need to choose five of you to be part of the school choir. So, we're going to start at the front of the coach and, if you're interested, you may audition. Just say 'no thank you' if you would prefer not to be in the choir."

She turned to Harvey and James who, once again, occupied the front seat. "Harvey, you go first," she said, passing him the microphone. "Why don't you start with 'Sleigh bells ring, are you listening?'"

Despite the knowledge that singing was not his forte, Harvey decided to give it his best effort. He took a deep breath and belted out the first line. Moans and groans erupted throughout the coach.

Miss Loveday held up her hand for everyone to stop. "Let's all try to be respectful. Harvey, thank you for being willing to participate and for your…um…enthusiasm. It would appear that your strengths lie elsewhere. I'm also responsible for selecting people for various speaking parts. A speaking part might be better for you." She looked down at her sheet. "King Herod would be a good fit. Are you okay with that?"

"Yes, Miss. I would love to be King Herod," he replied before passing back the mic. Harvey had seen Jack play the role of King Herod a few years before. The crown that was used for the part of King Herod was one of the more impressive props in the school's prop collection, and as a six-year-old, Harvey had fancied himself wearing it. He would get to live out one of his childhood dreams.

"Lovely. So we have our King Herod. I'm sure you will look smashing in that crown. Now how about you, James? Do you want to audition?"

"No thanks, Miss. I think I would do better with a non-singing part as well."

"Excellent. You would make a fine shepherd." She turned to the back of the coach. "Is there anyone who would actually *like* to audition for a singing part?" Several hands shot up. "Okay Ryan, you can come and join me at the front."

Ryan Jenkins sang "God rest ye merry gentlemen" surprisingly well, and Molly Pinker's Latin version of "Oh Come all Ye Faithful" was as incredible as everyone expected it to be. When Molly was done, Harvey tuned out the auditions and turned his attention towards James, who was frantically searching through his backpack for something.

"Did you lose something?" Harvey asked.

"I'm looking for anything that I might have forgotten to eat."

"What about that Yop?" he said, pointing to a bottle in James' backpack. "Yop has protein in it. That should help a bit."

"That's empty. I drank that on the way to school this morning."

"Have you tried squeezing it?"

"What's that going to do? You can't squeeze Yop out of an empty bottle."

"Try squeezing anyway and see what happens."

James took the Yop from the backpack. "I *know* what's going to happen," he said but squeezed the bottle anyway. The result was a loud pop as the bottle lid shot forwards like a rocket, striking the front windscreen of the coach and startling the driver. The whole coach shook as the driver swerved towards the kerb.

"What on earth are you boys up to?" Mr Hawking bellowed.

"We were doing the *second R*, sir," said Harvey. "We were reusing the bottle to help save the earth."

"What's that, Ranger? Speak up, boy! You know I am almost deaf in my left ear."

Harvey knew that Mr Hawking was almost deaf in one ear, but he hadn't previously clued in to the fact it was his left.

"The second R, sir," Harvey repeated, much louder this time. "We were doing the second 'R' to help save the environment. You know, *Reduce, Reuse, Recycle.*"

"Startling the driver could cause a crash and turn us all into organ donors, Ranger. Maybe *you* want your organs recycled, but I would prefer to keep using mine for many more years." Mr Hawking sat back down with a loud huff.

"He seems a little more bent out of shape than usual," James observed.

Harvey wasn't paying much attention. He was wondering why Mr Hawking was deaf in his left ear, and if perhaps Mr Hawking had ever played the bagpipes.

The rest of the drive home was spent auditioning for the choir, assigning parts in the play, and sharing a large Toblerone bar. The Toblerone was supplied by Molly Pinker, who was not only the best singer but had also won the colouring contest and decided to share her prize with the entire class. Even though it was an almost-four-hour drive back to the school, it certainly didn't feel like it to Class 6B of Weybourne College.

Chapter 16

BRAT DIET

Harvey went to sleep quickly that night, but it was only a few hours later when he woke up. His stomach felt most uncomfortable. He lay there for a minute, hoping the feeling would go away, but with every passing minute he began to feel more and more nauseous. It soon became apparent that he was going to be sick, and a sprint to the bathroom would be necessary. Harvey was just able to make it before the forces of nature took over, and he brought up much of the contents of his stomach. He lay down again, but the same thing happened an hour later and then again every few hours throughout the night.

By the time morning came, things were starting to improve, but even a small amount of breakfast resurfaced within a few minutes. There was no way Harvey was going to be able to go to school.

"Harvey, I'm *sure* you have food poisoning," said his mother. "Did you eat anything yesterday other than your packed lunch and the extra cheese and Marmite sandwich?"

"James and I bought a hot dog from a food cart," replied Harvey. "It didn't seem very hot, but we were hungry and the man running the cart was a bit scary, so we didn't dare complain."

"I'm going to call James' mother to see how he's doing."

Mrs Ranger returned a few minutes later.

"James was sick most of the night too. It was almost certainly the hot dogs that made you sick."

* * *

After a day of resting and just sipping water, Harvey was starting to feel a little better.

"I'm thinking we should start you on a BRAT diet," Mrs Ranger said.

"What's a BRAT diet?" Harvey asked.

"Bananas, rice, applesauce and toast," she explained.

Harvey ate some mashed banana on a piece of toast and then went to the living room to lie on the sofa. It wasn't long before he was fast asleep.

Chapter 17

SLIME THERAPY

It was well after tea time when Sally came bursting into the living room and started singing in a very shrill voice. "Slime, slime, I love slime. It's sublime all the time. Slime is good, slime is the best. Slime will give you a hairy chest!"

Needless to say, the trauma to Harvey's ears caused him to awaken. "Sally, stop," he moaned. You're giving me a headache, you stinker."

Sally looked surprised. "What's wrong? Don't you like slime?"

"It's not that," said Harvey. "It's your *singing*. It's horrendous, and you're killing my eardrums, and I bet you don't even know what sublime means."

Harvey knew a lot of clever words for an eleven-year-old, but he wasn't completely sure *he* knew what sublime meant. If he didn't know what it meant, it was pretty unlikely Sally would know. Harvey, however, was not aware that Sally had just been in the kitchen asking their mum for words rhyming with slime. When her mum had said, "sublime," Sally had asked what that meant. "Awe-inspiring and grand," her mother had told her, and that was exactly how Sally felt about her wonderful creations, having spent most of the evening perfecting her craft.

"Awe-inspiring and grand," she now said in response to Harvey's comment.

Harvey's jaw dropped. "Seriously? Where did you come up with that answer?"

"I'm just clever," Sally said. "Here, play with some. It will help you relax and get rid of your headache." She passed Harvey a giant blob of freshly made blue slime before sitting down on the armrest of the sofa.

Harvey held the slime in his hands. He squeezed it and stretched it and wrapped it back around on itself. Sally was right. It really was quite relaxing.

They spent the next few minutes stretching, twisting, and flopping the slime until it occurred to Harvey that the slime might stick to the walls or ceiling. From the sofa, he launched some red slime at the ceiling, where, to his delight, it stuck for about twenty seconds before coming unstuck and dropping back into his waiting hands.

"That's brilliant," said Harvey. "Let's try that again." He picked up the white blob. It was by far the largest and the stickiest. With all the strength he could muster, he flung it at the ceiling, where it stuck with a splat.

They both stared at the ceiling waiting for the slime to drop, but it didn't look like it was going anywhere.

"Do you think it will be stuck there forever?" Sally asked.

"Doubt it," replied Harvey. "It'll come down at some point when it's dried out enough. Good thing it's white. If it doesn't come down for a while, Mum and Dad might not notice it against the white ceiling."

"I hope your headache has gone away now. Throwing slime at the ceiling must have been very relaxing for you."

"Yes, I think so."

"You see, the slime really helped."

"It might have been the slime, but it's more likely the fact that you're no longer torturing my..." Not wanting to hurt his sister's feelings, Harvey cut himself short.

Sally chose to ignore him. "When you're feeling well enough to get off the sofa, you can come and buy some slime from my slime shop," she said.

Chapter 18

HISTORY REPEATS

Before Harvey could respond to Sally's invitation to visit her slime shop, their mum walked into the room, looking very well put together in one of her fashionable outfits. She stopped right under the great, white slime. Harvey and Sally looked up anxiously. If the slime dropped on their mum's head, it would be hilarious, but how would she react? They both made sure they didn't look at it.

"How are you feeling, Harvey?" Mrs Ranger inquired. "Do you need me to bring you some more applesauce?"

"No thanks, Mum. I'll just wait a little longer."

"Well, it's time for the news. Who's got the remote?"

Harvey extracted the remote from the crack between the cushions of the sofa and turned on the TV. Mrs Ranger sat down on the couch by Harvey's feet, and they started to watch the news. There was a story about new lines being painted on the Tesco car park that were supposed to make things safer for pedestrians and another about plans to enlarge the size of the boathouse for the Royal National Lifeboat Institution's lifeboat. Apparently the new lifeboat was one metre too long to fit in the existing boathouse. Lifeboats fascinated Harvey, but road markings not so much.

However, the next story had Harvey on full alert. There had been another sighting of a humpback whale. This time the sighting was just east of Portland, but no more details were given before the words *BREAKING NEWS* started to scroll across the bottom of the screen in large red letters. The camera cut to a female reporter standing in front of the Tower of London.

"There has been a major incident at the Tower of London today. We now go to a live press conference with Police Commissioner Nigel Bean, the head of Scotland Yard, as he explains in more detail what has happened."

Nigel Bean appeared on the TV. He was standing in front of a bank of microphones.

Harvey listened intently as the police commissioner described what had taken place:

"Just a short while ago, a large gang of thieves overcame the guards and security personnel at the Tower of London and stole the Crown Jewels. The thieves were all dressed in parson robes and claimed to be members of a bagpipe band called The Piping Parsons. This band was scheduled to perform in a national talent show tomorrow but had booked a private, after-hours viewing of the crown jewels for this evening. Shortly after the tour started, one of the members of the band appeared to be having a heart attack. An ambulance was called. As soon as the ambulance arrived, members of the thirty-man band pulled weapons from under their parson robes. The Yeomen on duty were forced to unlock the display cases before being tied up and gagged with all the other security personnel. The Crown Jewels were loaded into the ambulance, which left the Tower of London with siren blaring. It is interesting to note that the robbery has similarities to a failed attempt by Thomas Blood to steal the Crown Jewels in 1671.

"We currently have in place one of the largest manhunts in history. We are watching for any suspicious activity at seaports and airports around the country, and there are numerous roadblocks in and around the London area. We will catch the individuals responsible for this crime, and they will be held accountable."

The camera cut away from the chief of the police and focused on the news anchor, who announced, "And now we are going to go live with the prime minister, who wishes to address the nation."

The prime minister came on the TV looking rather sombre and wearing a black jacket and pants. She was adjusting some papers on the podium in front of her.

"Oh dear," said Mrs Ranger, "that suit she's wearing today is a bit frumpy, and it really doesn't suit her lovely personality. She's a beautiful woman, but her clothes work against her. One day I would love to visit her at Number 10 to do a wardrobe consultation."

"What's Number 10?" Sally asked.

"It's where the prime minister lives, sweetie," said Mrs Ranger. "It's short for her address of 10 Downing Street, Westminster, London."

Mrs Ranger stopped as the prime minister looked up and started to speak.

"As you have already heard, a brazen gang of thugs has stolen the Crown Jewels. I have assured the queen that all police and security forces are working hard to make sure the jewels are recovered. As you probably know, the value of the jewels is more than just monetary. They are also a national treasure with a history going back over six hundred years. The only previous attempt to steal the jewels was in 1671, and that attempt failed. We believe this attempt will also fail. I urge members of the public to look out for *anything* unusual. We have set up a hotline for anyone to call with tips. If you see *anything* that is out of the ordinary, please call the hotline at the number displayed on the screen below."

Chapter 19

OUT OF THE ORDINARY

Jack walked into the room as the prime minister finished making her statement. He was followed by Radar, who was looking scruffy as usual. While loved dearly by his young owner, Radar had few redeeming qualities. From the more sensitive members of society, his appearance and odour usually solicited the polite comment, "Oh, isn't he an extraordinary dog?"

The extraordinary dog's owner flopped himself down in an armchair. "What's going on?" asked Jack.

"Someone's stolen the crown jewels," replied Sally matter-of-factly. She looked down at Radar who stood there looking around the room at everyone, trying to figure out what was going on.

With a sly grin on her face, Sally grabbed a pencil and a piece of paper and wrote down the phone number on the screen. She immediately picked up the cordless phone and started to dial the number. Everyone looked at her in surprise. "Sally, what are you doing?" said her mother.

"I'm calling the hotline to tell the prime minister about Radar," she said.

"But why do you want to tell the prime minister about Radar?" said Mrs Ranger, looking surprised.

"Because he isn't an ordinary dog, and the prime minister said to call if we saw anything out of the ordinary," she replied.

"Sally, you stinker. Hang up the phone," said her mother. "Radar didn't steal the Crown Jewels and you know it."

Radar gave a quick woof at the mention of his name and looked at Mrs Ranger. She patted him on the head. Despite Harvey's weakened condition, he could not help himself from laughing out loud.

"No wonder Harvey's on a BRAT diet," said Sally. "He's such a brat."

"That reminds me. Harvey," said Mrs Ranger. "Let's get you something else to eat and then get you up to your bed. And Jack, Radar is rather smelly again. Please give him a bath, or he'll be banned from the house."

"Tomorrow, mum," said Jack. "I'll give him a bath in the morning. I've got Jasper tonight."

"Didn't you just go to Jasper yesterday morning?" said Harvey. "What's so terribly interesting about rocks and minerals?"

"Jasper really rocks," said Jack with a grin. "You should come sometime."

"No thanks," said Harvey, "I'd rather spend another night vomiting my guts out."

Having finished his toast, Harvey dragged himself up the stairs to bed.

The big blob of white slime that clung to the ceiling was long forgotten.

Chapter 20

RESTLESS NIGHT

Before lying down, Harvey picked up the booklet Yeoman Nick had handed out at the end of the tour. He pulled a black marker from the drawer in his bedside table. *Towers* of London, he said to himself as he used the marker to add an *s* after *Tower*. At least now *his* copy of the booklet was accurate.

Harvey opened the booklet and flipped through the pages, stopping at the story of The Princes in the Tower. The two most popular explanations for the princes' disappearance were discussed in the article, along with the third, less popular, theory that the younger prince, Richard Duke of York, had escaped from The Tower of London and fled to Belgium.

This is what Mr Hawking was talking about during the tour, Harvey realised. The theory was based on the fact that a man from Belgium called Perkin Warbeck claimed that he was actually Richard Duke of York. He was able to convince a lot of people he was the prince and therefore that he should be the king in his older brother's absence. He went to England in an attempt to seize the throne for himself but was defeated. Eventually, Perkin Warbeck was executed by King Henry the Seventh, but not before having a son in England.

What happened to his son? Harvey wondered. *If Perkin Warbeck was really the prince, then he should have been king and his son after him. What if our family was descended from the Warbecks and Dad was king. That would make me a prince and people would have to call me Sir Harvey...even Mr Hawking would have to call me Sir.* And with those jumbled thoughts still drifting around in his head, he drifted off to sleep.

* * *

Nearly seven hours after going to sleep, Harvey woke up. He checked the time on his watch: 3:02 a.m. He rolled over and tried to go back to sleep. *Alpha, Bravo, Charlie, Delta, Foxtrot,* he whispered to himself. Harvey preferred the phonetic alphabet to counting sheep, but this time even this strategy wasn't working.

As he lay there staring at the ceiling, his mind started to wander to the news story about the Crown Jewels, and that reminded him of the other news story about the humpback sighted just east of Portland. *If the whale was just east of Portland, then it was almost in Weymouth Bay. What if the whale was in Weymouth Bay right now?*

Harvey quietly climbed out of bed and opened the window. The Ranger house sat on the top of a small cliff with the back of the house facing southeast over the bay. On a clear day, Harvey could see most of Weymouth Bay, but this was night-time and clouds were blocking the waxing crescent moon. Harvey couldn't see much from the window except the lights on the four breakwaters that outlined Portland Harbour and, further in the distance, the lights from the Isle of Portland. But light shining off the water told him one thing; the water was calm and this meant there was little wind.

Portland Harbour was naturally protected on three sides, but the eastern side was protected by the four man-made breakwaters. There were numerous buildings on the breakwaters, including a fort and other structures that had been built as defensive measures during the various wars. The lights on these buildings served as a warning to ships. The most northern breakwater, the one closest to the Ranger home, was called Bincleaves Groyne. The buildings on it had, at one time, been used in the development and testing of torpedoes and sonar. Now, they were mostly derelict.

Harvey walked back across the room to the foot of Jack's bed and grabbed Jack's binoculars from the hook where they had been hanging. Radar woke up and followed Harvey as he returned to the window. Harvey bent over and rubbed Radar's head. "Quiet Radar," he whispered. He raised the binoculars to his eyes and scanned the bay to the east, but the binoculars were no better than his naked eye. *It figures, nothing is still nothing even when you get a closer look at it.* Harvey scanned along the length of Bincleaves Groyne, stopping at the short-range torpedo test building.

The building sat on a pier jutting out from the breakwater, roughly two hundred and fifty metres from the shoreline. Harvey noticed there were some lights on, which didn't surprise him too much. Mr Ranger had mentioned at breakfast a couple of weeks ago that this building had been leased to a company called SAG Upholstery. Apparently, SAG was in the business of commercial furniture updating and repairing and, having signed a large contract with a short deadline, were working around the clock to get things done. "Unfortunate name for an upholstery business," Mrs Ranger had said at the time.

With nothing more exciting to observe than lights in a window, Harvey decided to go back to bed. As he turned around, he saw his backpack on the floor. He remembered his Buzzbird 400 drone hadn't been unpacked since the trip to the Tower and, thanks to Mr Hawking who didn't let him take the drone to London, the battery would be almost fully charged.

A thought popped into Harvey's head. The drone was smaller than the window, and the drone's camera had night vision capabilities. He could fly the drone right out the window and over the bay to search for the whale without ever leaving his room.

Harvey set the binoculars on the floor, slowly unzipped his backpack and removed the Buzzbird 400. He turned the drone on, grabbed the controller, and put on his FPV goggles.

There were three cameras attached to the bottom of the drone, all mounted in a camera pod. The view from the forward-looking camera took up most of the top of the FPV display, and the two side-looking cameras each covered half of the lower portion of the screen. Overlaid on the display was all the information that Harvey needed to know about the drone's altitude, speed, battery level and GPS location. When the GPS indicator went green, meaning it had received signals from enough satellites to triangulate its location, Harvey was ready to fly.

"Radar, come here," whispered Harvey. With the FPV goggles covering his eyes he wasn't able to see anything around him, and he wanted to make sure Radar wouldn't be hurt by the spinning blades. He felt Radar brush against his leg. He reached down and patted his head once more. It was time to fly.

Harvey pushed the left stick of the controller forwards and the blades of the drone started spinning with a loud whirring, buzzing sound. If Jack was going to wake up, this would be the moment. He needed to act quickly. Pushing the right stick forward, he flew the drone out the window.

Jack rolled over in bed, and in a panicked voice he mumbled, "Get away. Get away. Noooo!"

Harvey stood still, waiting to see what would happen next.

When Jack spoke again, it was with a normal whisper. "You awake, Harvey?"

"Yeah, what's going on?" Harvey feigned a sleepy voice.

"I thought I was being attacked by a swarm of angry bees."

By this time, the drone was out of earshot, having passed over the cliff at the end of the garden.

"Angry bees?" replied Harvey, stifling a laugh. "I don't hear angry bees. Are you sure you're not losing it?"

"I'm not losing it. I just had the most vivid nightmare of my entire life. The sound was so real," Jack said before rolling over again and falling back to sleep.

After flying a short distance over the water, Harvey changed course and headed east. He figured it was less likely there would be whales in Portland Harbour, so he would head for the open bay.

A minute later, he was adjacent to the SAG building. Needless to say, the temptation to spy through the windows was more than just fleeting, but Harvey wasn't the nosy type and furniture upholstery was way less exciting than whale watching. He continued flying east and watched as Bincleaves Groyne passed beneath him.

With a fully charged battery, the Buzzbird 400, under normal circumstances, could fly for fifty-five kilometres. With the battery slightly used from doing the group shot before the school trip, Harvey figured the range would be more like fifty kilometres. He did some quick maths in his head. He was already a kilometre from home. The drone had a radio range of just over six kilometres, likely only five with the walls of the house reducing the signal, so he would conduct a grid search by flying four kilometres into the bay and four kilometres back a total of five times. He turned on the latitude and longitude indicator on the FPV display and started to fly directly east, following a fixed line of longitude with a heading of ninety degrees. *This was going to be fun.*

During the first pass, there wasn't much to see: just water and a few seagulls, but no whales. When he reached a point that was four kilometres from where he'd crossed over the breakwater, Harvey turned right ninety degrees and flew for one hundred metres towards the open sea before turning right again and completing a return pass on a path parallel to the first pass. This pass was also completed without spotting any whales or whitecaps, or anything at all.

At this point, it occurred to Harvey that he didn't need to be standing any longer, so he felt with his hand for the edge of the bed and lay down. *Oh, the wonders of technology*, he thought. *Here I am lying in my bed in the middle of the night while searching for whales at the same time.*

Chapter 21

THE WHALE THAT WASN'T

Harvey was beginning to wonder if the whale search was a lost cause. He'd completed two round trips into the bay and had not seen a single whale. He decided to try just a little longer.

He had just started the third pass when something on his screen caught his eye. He sent the drone into a dive to get a closer look. The object was long and round on top and shaped like a whale. "Jack, Jack!" Harvey cried out. "I've found a whale! There's a whale in the bay."

"You're just dreaming," mumbled Jack. "No one's spotted a whale in Weymouth Bay in a bazillion years. Even if there were a whale in the bay, you wouldn't be able to see it from your bed. Go back to sleep."

Harvey flew lower to get a better look. As he got closer, he saw something sticking out of the top of the whale that made him think it wasn't a whale after all. "It's not a dream," said Harvey excitedly. "It's a submarine!"

The camera had been zoomed out to a wide angle for the whale search, making Harvey think that the submarine was further away than it actually was. If it hadn't been for a last-second swerve to the right, the drone would have smashed into the conning tower, which stuck out of the top of the submarine. The drone got so close, Harvey could see the surprised look on the face of a man whose head appeared at the top of the tower.

The man in the tower wasn't the only one who was surprised. Even though Harvey only saw his face for a split second, he was sure there was something familiar about it.

"I almost crashed into the conning tower, and I think I recognised that man from somewhere," Harvey told Jack.

"You're the one losing it," said Jack. "You've completely lost your marbles. You're probably suffering delusions from dehydration. Have some water and go back to sleep."

"I'm not delusional, Jack. Ask me a question that a delusional person couldn't answer."

"Alright. What's your name, rank and serial number?"

"My name is Harvey Ranger and I'm not in the army so I don't have a rank or serial number."

"I still think you're bonkers," Jack muttered.

Harvey knew the rule about operating drones too close to other vehicles, but this was an unusual situation that warranted some further investigation. He decided to ignore Jack and the rules for the time being and swung around for another look. The drone started to approach the submarine from the port side. Harvey pressed the record button on the controller so he would have a video record of what he had seen.

As the drone got closer, Harvey could see that the man in the conning tower had something in his hand. His heart skipped a beat. "He's got a machine gun!" yelled Harvey. "And he's shooting at me. I can see the muzzle flash." To Harvey, it almost seemed like the man was shooting right at his face. Harvey pulled a sharp right turn and started to climb, but the display suddenly went dark. "I can't believe it! He just shot down my drone."

Jack sat up. "So let's get this straight," he said. "You saw a whale that turned out to be a submarine. There's a man in the submarine that you might recognize. The man used the machine gun to shoot down your drone. And you expect me to believe that you aren't delusional?"

Before Harvey could respond, the distant but distinct rat-tat-tat-tat sound of a machine gun could be heard through the open window.

Jack jumped out of bed. "Did you hear that? It sounded like a machine gun!"

"That's because it was a machine gun," Harvey insisted. "And that proves I'm not delusional."

"At least no more delusional than normal," Jack quipped, moving towards Harvey. "The sound arrived almost ten seconds after you said he was shooting at you. Sound travels at roughly three hundred and forty metres per second. So if it was ten seconds, then your friend with the machine gun is nearly three and a half kilometres away."

"Wow, it's amazing that we can hear gunshots at that distance," said Harvey.

"Sound does strange things over water at night. The cooler air on the water's surface causes the sound waves to bend downward with a focusing effect. It's a bit like a mirage in the desert, only that's with light and this is sound. Are you absolutely sure it was a submarine and not a boat?"

"I'm positive it was a submarine. A small one. It couldn't have been any longer than ten or fifteen metres, which is why I thought it was a whale."

"Why would there be a submarine in Weymouth Bay, I wonder?" Jack stood up and started pacing the floor. "The Royal Navy left Portland Harbour in the nineties, and I don't even think they have any subs that are that small. Maybe it's some type of research sub."

"Who would be researching the impact of machine gun fire from submarines, on small drones, in the middle of the night?" Harvey turned off the controller and took off his goggles. "I can't believe I just lost another drone," he sighed. "It'll take months to earn enough money to replace it. And that video footage is lost as well."

"I'm sorry about your drone." Jack sat on the bed next to Harvey. "I just wish I knew what that sub was doing in the bay. Was the man wearing a navy uniform?"

"No. It looked like he was wearing a dark robe or something like that, and he had long hair. I'd say this would definitely be classified as out of the ordinary."

"We need to call the hotline," Jack said.

"I think the piece of paper Sally wrote the number on is still on the coffee table."

Jack got up from his bed and tiptoed hurriedly downstairs. He came back a minute later with the piece of paper and a phone in his hand. He quickly dialled the number. The phone was answered by an automated attendant. Jack put the phone on speaker so Harvey could hear as well.

"Thank you for calling the Crown Jewels hotline. Unfortunately, we are still following up on a large number of leads, and there is no one available to speak with you at the moment. Please leave a detailed message after the beep."

Jack hung up the phone.

"Wow, they're so overwhelmed with tips they can't even answer the phone," said Harvey. "It must be all the people calling in about their extraordinary dogs. We'll have to try something else. Let's call 9-9-9."

Jack dialled 9-9-9. A woman's voice answered the phone. "Emergency services. Do you require police, fire or ambulance?"

"Police," said Jack.

A man's voice came on the phone next. "This is the police service. How can we assist you?"

"My brother was looking for whales in Weymouth Bay with his drone. At first, he thought he had found one, but it turned out it wasn't a whale–it was a submarine. We think it's suspicious and want to report it." Jack's words spilled out as he did his best to describe the situation.

"Look, 9-9-9 is for serious calls only, son. Please don't waste our time," came the reply.

"But I *am* serious. And a man in the submarine shot down my brother's drone."

"Okay, we'll send someone in the morning," the man responded.

Jack provided their home address and then hung up. "That's no use," he said, shaking his head. "That sub could be a hundred kilometres away by morning."

Chapter 22

MR RANGER MAKES A CALL

Harvey and Jack hadn't realised, but as their excitement increased so had the volume of their voices. The Ranger home was an older home with thick walls, but the boys had still made enough noise to wake up their mum and dad.

The door opened, and both parents walked in. "What's going on?" asked Mr Ranger. "It's the middle of the night."

"There's a submarine in the bay," said Harvey excitedly.

"And it shot down his drone," Jack added.

"Maybe you had a nightmare," suggested their mum, looking puzzled.

"I heard the sounds of the gun too," said Jack. "So unless we had the same dream, it wasn't a dream."

"What was your drone doing over Weymouth Bay at three-thirty in the morning?" asked Mr Ranger.

"I couldn't get back to sleep, and I wanted to have another look for that humpback."

"We'll talk more about that later." By this time, the fog had cleared from Mr Ranger's head and the things Harvey was saying were starting to activate a part of his brain that had been developed over many years of training with MI5. "Tell us about the submarine, Harvey. How big was it? Were there any markings on the side?"

"I'm not sure about markings, but it did seem smaller than subs you would normally expect to see the navy using. At first, I was really excited because I thought I'd spotted a whale."

"Can you remember anything else about the sub? Anything at all?"

"There was a man..." was all Harvey said in response, as something outside the window drew his attention. He stared, mouth open, towards the end of the garden. Sure enough, he could see the blinking lights of his drone. The lights were followed by the familiar buzzing sound of the four electric motors.

Everyone turned to look as the Buzzbird 400 flew in through the open window and landed on the floor.

"It wasn't shot *down* after all!" Harvey exclaimed. "It's programmed to fly itself home when it loses contact with the controller."

He got up from his bed and picked up the drone. "Look, the camera has a bullet hole right through it." He pointed to the hole in the camera pod. "But it looks like the bullet missed the memory card slot! There should be a video of the sub on the card. Let's go to RISC, and I'll pull the images up on my computer."

The four Rangers proceeded down the hall and entered the door with the sign that read *Enter at your own RISC.* Otherwise known as Ranger Information Systems Centre, RISC was the reason Jack and Harvey shared a room. It was Harvey's brainchild. The idea was conceived after Mr Ranger declared that electronic devices with screens of all types did not belong in bedrooms. It was once Harvey's bedroom but was now the room in which both Harvey and Jack had a desk, shared printers, and scanners. On the shelves were an assortment of drones, model aeroplanes, and Jack's athletic trophies. The walls were adorned with newspaper clippings of Harvey's previous escapades and pictures of Jack posing with his trophies.

Harvey sat down at his desk, removed the memory card from the drone, and inserted it into the card reader on his laptop. The others gathered around Harvey's desk to watch as he opened the video file. There were three windows in the video feed matching the view from the goggles. The two smaller ones at the bottom were for the left and right-facing cameras, and the top one was for the forward-facing camera. All eyes were focussed on the top screen, which showed the sub as the drone approached it.

"If I'm not mistaken," said Mr Ranger, "that is a Swedish Spiggen II midget sub. They were retired a few years back. It looks like someone may have purchased one and repurposed it."

In the video, the drone was getting closer to the sub.

"Watch how close the drone gets to the man's face!" said Harvey. "It must have really startled him."

"He probably figured there was no chance in the world that there would be anyone about at that time," said Mr Ranger. "Look at what he's wearing. He's definitely not in the navy. It looks like he's dressed in something a vicar or priest would wear."

"Maybe a parson's cloak?" said Harvey. "Like the ones the Piping Parsons were wearing when they stole the Crown Jewels."

"You're quite right. Well done, Harvey," said Mr Ranger. "Let's get another look at him."

Harvey replayed the video and hit pause when the drone was at the closest point to the man.

"Arched nose and a prominent chin," said Mr Ranger. "I'm pretty sure I recognize this character. If I'm not mistaken, that is Smelliwig. He runs a large crime syndicate, and the police have been looking for him for years. He's been known to commit copycat crimes in the past. It seems that this time, he's copying Thomas Blood and trying to steal the Crown Jewels. It's too bad we can't get a better view of his eyes. One of them is blue and the other is brown."

"I think I recognise him too," said Harvey.

Everyone turned to look at him in surprise.

"He looks like the man who sold us the hot dog at the Towers of London."

"Well that would make sense," said Mr Ranger. "He was probably using the hot dog cart as a cover for staking out The Tower. He would have been watching the movement of the guards."

Suddenly Jack exclaimed, "Back that video up a bit, Harvey! I think I saw something from one of the side cameras."

Harvey replayed the video.

"Stop! Look there," said Jack, pointing to the screen. "There's a boat."

Sure enough, a small fishing boat with three men on board could be seen in the lower left screen.

"And on the deck," said Mr Ranger, "see those large coolers? They could easily hold something like the Crown Jewels."

"And look at the man driving the boat," Harvey added. "He seems much stockier than the others. He reminds me of the Tank guy we saw on the whale watching trip." Harvey caught himself, remembering that he wasn't supposed to say anything about his dad being on the boat. "I mean, who *I* saw on the whale watching trip. You all saw him in the video."

"Good eye," said Mr Ranger. "I can tell you one thing for sure. He won't be boarding the submarine. There's room for six on that sub, but there's little room to move around."

Jack slapped his brother on the back. "Well done, Harvey. You've caught the thieves. You're going to be famous!"

"Let's not jump to any conclusions," cautioned Mrs Ranger. "We don't know for sure yet what's going on out there, and even if it is the Crown Jewels, they still have to be recovered."

"I'm going to make a phone call," said Mr Ranger, "and we're going to find out what that sub is up to. I'll need those GPS coordinates from the video feed."

Harvey wrote the coordinates down on a piece of paper and passed it to his dad, who immediately left the room. With his MI5 connections, Reginald Ranger had direct access to some very influential people, the kind who were in a position to make things happen quickly.

Jack smiled at his younger brother. "I wasn't imagining the sound of angry bees, was I?"

"No," admitted Harvey, "you weren't. Sorry about that."

Chapter 23

THE DRONE RANGER

"I spoke to some people at the MOD," said Mr Ranger upon his return to RISC. "They're sending helicopters from the Coast Guard, the National Police Air Service, and the Royal Navy. The Coast Guard chopper was returning from another call and is already in the air, so it will arrive first. The police chopper will arrive shortly after. The problem is that neither of those choppers is going to be equipped with sonar, and without sonar, they won't be able to see into the water to find the sub. The navy will have sonar, but they won't arrive for nearly an hour. By that time, the sub will almost certainly be gone. We need something that has sonar, and we need it now." He looked directly at Harvey.

"I have sonar on my Buzzbird 550S drone," Harvey said.

"You have a sonar-equipped drone?" said Mr Ranger with mock surprise.

Harvey spoke frequently and with great detail about his drones, so the merits of the various models were well known to his family members. Still, that didn't stop him from doing a recap just in case someone had forgotten.

"It's the hexacopter drone the navy gave me as a thank-you gift when I saved Petty Officer Flopbottom from drowning. It can float on water and has a sonar fish finder, remember? It can detect a five-kilogram fish at two hundred metres, fly at up to sixty kilometres per hour, and stay in the air for forty minutes. It also has an infrared camera and can lift a one-kilogram load."

"Well, you certainly deserved it, Harvey," Mr Ranger said. "It would have been Officer Flopbottom's last day, if you hadn't been about your wits and used your drone to deliver him that empty plastic bottle so he could stay afloat." Mr Ranger put his arm around Harvey's shoulder. "We have one shot at catching this sub, and you and your fish-finding drone are it. You haven't eaten much since Thursday. Do you think you're up for it?"

Harvey's body wasn't being fuelled by the usual assortment of bacon, eggs, chips, chicken pie, and roast potatoes that made up his regular diet. These had left his system long ago, and now there were only trace amounts of applesauce and toast left to keep him going. Fortunately the traces of applesauce and toast were starting to get some help from adrenaline.

"I'm fine, Dad. I feel like I have lots of energy. I know I can do it," he said.

"Well then, let's get cracking. It won't take the thieves long to transfer the jewels from the boat to the sub."

Harvey walked across the room to where the Buzzbird 550S was hanging on the wall. "It'll take me a few minutes to get the drone ready and outside. This one's too big to fly out the window." He took the drone down from where it was hanging on the wall and set it on the floor. After inserting a fresh battery, he placed a spare in his pocket, along with his phone. "Once the drone's in the air, it should be at the sub's location in about three minutes," he explained.

Jack helped Harvey by carrying the FPV goggles and controller to the back of the house. It was still a beautiful, calm night. Harvey was struck by how quiet it was with so few cars on the roads and no birds chirping. In the excitement of the moment, it seemed as if he could hear his own heart beating. He didn't feel tired or weak. The adrenaline was doing its job.

Harvey placed the drone on the ground, and Jack passed him the controller.

"You can do this," Jack said. "The navy, coast guard and police can't catch these guys in time, but Harvey the Drone Ranger can."

"Thanks," Harvey grinned as he placed the FPV goggles over his head and gripped the controller. "Now, could you read me the coordinates from that piece of paper?"

He punched in the GPS coordinates for the destination as Jack read them out to him and then waited for the drone to lock in the GPS satellite signals. Once the GPS location was confirmed, Harvey launched his drone into the air and headed back to the last known location of the submarine.

Chapter 24

SPECIAL DELIVERY TO BINCLEAVES GREEN

"Dad, are you sure this plan is going to work? Will the fish finder be able to locate a submarine?" Harvey asked as the second drone passed over Bincleaves Groyne.

"If your drone can detect a five-kilogram fish at a depth of two hundred metres, then it's going to be able to detect an eleven-metre, fourteen-thousand-kilogram submarine at a depth of twenty metres."

"Why twenty metres?" said Harvey.

"That sub is at least twenty-five years old. I'm assuming they haven't been maintaining it properly. Would you dive deeper than you had to in a twenty-five-year-old, poorly maintained sub?"

"No. But why even go down twenty metres?"

"There are many ships in the channel, so they'll want to dive down deep enough to avoid a collision," said Mr Ranger. "Do you see that sub yet?"

"Yes, I see it. I have the camera zoomed out, and I can just see the sub now. The boat is pulling away, and the sub looks like it's moving forward and now…now it's starting to dive. We made it!"

"Fantastic! Keep your eye on the spot where it goes under and try landing on the water roughly thirty metres in front of that spot. You should be able to pick up the sub on your fish finder."

Harvey continued to fly the Buzzbird 550S at top speed towards the spot in the water where he had last seen the submarine. After reaching the spot, he flew on another thirty metres and landed. "Drone's in the water," he announced. "Activating sonar."

Harvey, Jack, and Mr Ranger waited with bated breath.

"I can't see it, Dad," Harvey said. "The whole screen is dark."

"Don't worry. Maybe you're sitting smack dab on top of the sub so that the sub fills the entire display. Try flying ahead another thirty metres. They'll dive deeper as they move forward."

Using the distance from home indicator as a reference, Harvey flew the drone ahead another thirty metres, landed on the water, and then checked the sonar display.

"Okay, I've got it now. I see the front of the sub just coming into view on the sonar image. It's showing a depth of ten metres. After it passes underneath, I'll fly ahead another thirty metres and keep hopping along the surface like that."

Harvey focussed on flying for a moment, and then something came to mind. "Dad, what are we going to do when the drone is too far away? The controller's range is only about six kilometres."

"I'll work on solving that problem. You keep tracking the sub," said Mr Ranger as he pulled his phone from his pocket and started to make another call.

A couple of minutes later, he hung up the phone and said, "Harvey, you're going for a couple of rides. The first will be to Bincleaves Green in the box of the cargo bike. The second will be from Bincleaves Green, out over Weymouth Bay in the Coast Guard helicopter."

It took a moment for Harvey's mind to grasp what his dad was saying. It sounded too good to be true. "Do you mean to say I'll be riding in a chopper to keep up with the submarine?"

"That's right. You might be the first person in history to track a submarine with a drone while riding in a helicopter."

"Wow, Dad. This is serious business, isn't it?" said Harvey as his dad's words started to sink in.

* * *

Jack retrieved the cargo bike from the shed and brought it over to where Harvey and Mr Ranger were standing. The cargo bike, which was used to make deliveries for the bakery, had a large box up front. It had plenty of room for Harvey to sit in with his knees slightly bent.

"Let's get you in the box, Harvey," said Mr Ranger. "We need to arrive at the park before the Coast Guard."

Since Harvey was unable to see anything around him, Jack took hold of his arm and helped him into the cargo box. Harvey held onto the controller with one hand and used the other to steady himself as he sat on the bottom of the box, facing forward.

A few seconds later, Jack was breathlessly pedalling the cargo bike up Castle Bell Road with Harvey sitting up front, while Mr Ranger pedalled along beside them on his bike.

"The sub's going to be picking up speed to a maximum of ten kilometres per hour," said Mr Ranger. "Keep going with the thirty-metre hops. If you get too far ahead, then you'll need to reduce your hop length. Remember that the sub could change direction at any time, but it won't be able to turn so sharply that you'll lose sight of it."

"Thanks, Dad," responded Harvey as the *chuff-chuff-chuff* sound of the Coast Guard chopper could be heard approaching from a distance.

Chapter 25

UP, UP AND SIDEWAYS

Jack and Mr Ranger pulled the bikes up behind a large tree on the cliff side of Bincleaves Green. Mr Ranger removed the light from the front of his bike and stepped out into the open, using the light to signal the chopper. The chopper paused overhead, and two flood lights lit up the ground. The noise from the helicopter was deafening.

"I bet we're not the only ones awake now, Dad," yelled Jack above the noise.

"You're right about that," Mr Ranger replied. "Hopefully no one can see us well enough to recognise us. When the chopper lands, we'll come out from behind the trees and the chopper will be between us and most of the houses. If Smelliwig's plans fail, he's going to want to know why, so it's best to keep our identities hidden as much as possible."

"And I bet you don't want the neighbours to see you and Jack in your pyjamas," Harvey added. "You're probably both wishing you had slept in your clothes like me."

Harvey could feel the downwash from the chopper tugging at his clothes and hair as it touched down on the grass just twenty metres in front of him.

"Out you get, Harvey," Mr Ranger instructed. "You've got a flight to catch."

Jack helped Harvey stand up and steadied him as he stepped out of the cargo box. With Jack on one side of Harvey and his dad on the other, the trio slowly walked towards the helicopter.

They had just passed underneath the spinning rotors of the helicopter when Jack yelled out, "Break a leg, Harvey," and then released his grip on Harvey's arm. Almost immediately, Harvey felt another hand guiding him, where Jack's hand had been.

"Harvey, I'm Winchman Paramedic Hester Sturmey," shouted a woman's voice. "I'm going to be assisting you today." Hester guided Harvey up to the side of the chopper. She helped him climb aboard and into his seat next to the door, and then buckled him in.

"You can do this, Harvey! I'm proud of you," shouted Mr Ranger through the open door of the chopper.

"Thanks, Dad," Harvey shouted back as he focused intently on landing the drone on the water. Mr Ranger reached in and patted Harvey on the leg before running back behind the trees to join Jack.

Hester placed a headset over Harvey's ears so they wouldn't have to shout. With the headset on, Harvey could talk to the crew in the helicopter.

"Welcome aboard, Harvey," said the pilot. "My name's Captain Simon Jeeves, my co-pilot is Chris Jackman, and your winchmen for today are Alf Deacon and Hester Sturmey, whom you've already met. Are you still tracking that submarine?"

"Yes sir," Harvey replied. "It's just passing under my drone now with a heading of 102 degrees."

"All right, we're going to get ourselves airborne and then you can provide me with the coordinates," said Simon. "Harvey, you need to let us know if you need anything. Don't be afraid to speak up."

Hester closed the door of the helicopter, but before she sat down, Harvey called out, "I've lost contact with my drone. The drone's nearly four kilometres away. Shutting the door must have blocked the weak signal."

Hester immediately opened the door. "Door's open again," she said. "Are we back in business?"

"Thanks, that worked, but it's already flying home. It does that if it loses contact with the controller. I'm guessing it would have been flying home for about ten seconds, so I'll fly back for about twenty seconds before landing again." Harvey flew ahead to the spot where he anticipated the submarine would be and landed the drone.

Sure enough, the sub came into view almost immediately. "I see it again," he said. "Can you fly sideways with the door open?"

"Your wish is my command," said Simon. "But it's going to get draughty."

While Harvey flew the drone ahead on its next hop, he overheard the chatter between Simon and air traffic control. "This is Rescue One-oh-Five," Simon said. "We're ready to take off from Bincleaves Green in Weymouth."

"Rescue One-oh-Five, you're cleared for take-off," came the response from air traffic control. "What is your requested destination and altitude?"

"Requesting unrestricted access to air space over Weymouth Bay for emergency operations," said Simon. "We don't plan to exceed two hundred metres."

"Weymouth Bay is all yours, Rescue One-oh-Five. Do not exceed two hundred metres," responded air traffic control.

Harvey could feel the vibration as the chopper's engines started to pick up speed, and then, just as he lifted the drone off the water, the chopper began to rise into the air. The combined feeling of the chopper rising and the first-person view from the drone made Harvey feel like he was really flying. He reminded himself that he was, and smiled. *I can't believe this is happening*, he thought.

The night air was cool, and Harvey hadn't been warm to begin with. Now a blast of air was buffeting his body as Simon flew the helicopter sideways towards the location of the submarine. "A bit draughty was quite the understatement," he said. "This feels more like gale-force winds to me. I'll likely freeze to death in about a minute."

Hester wrapped a blanket around him. "There you go. We'll try to keep you alive for more than a minute."

There was some more radio chatter with air traffic control, and then Simon spoke to Harvey again. "Harvey, I need you to give me the current location of your drone."

Harvey read out the coordinates from his display and added, "The drone has a blinking red light, so you should be able to see it easily when we get closer."

"Thanks, Harvey." There was a pause, and then Simon said, "Well Harvey my lad, if your little submarine is going at ten kilometres per hour like your dad said it would, then we should catch up to it in just over ten minutes."

"That's great," said Harvey. "But don't get too close to the drone, or you'll blow it over. If it goes in the water upside down, it will float, but I won't be able to right it."

After ten minutes, Simon started to slow the chopper down, and Hester looked out the side door.

"I have a visual on the drone," she said. "I'm seeing a small blinking red light ahead and below. I think we're close enough."

Chapter 26

THE RAFT

Harvey completed another hop and then checked the drone's battery level. "The drone is spending about one-quarter of the time in the air and the rest of the time floating. At that pace, the battery should last at least another hour," he said.

"That's longer than we can stay out here," said Simon. "We have to clear out of here in less than twenty-eight minutes due to our fuel situation. The request to give you a ride came in while we were returning from another call. We're just a stop-gap solution. As it stands now, we won't be able to make it back to our base at Lee-on-Solent, so we're going to set her down in a field near Swanage. We'll wait there for a lorry to bring us some more fuel."

"But Swanage is too far for me," Harvey responded. "It'll be out of range for my drone. How are we going to catch the sub if we lose track of it?"

The co-pilot spoke for the first time. "Harvey, this is Chris Jackman, your co-pilot. At this point, we don't know how we're going to catch the sub. For now, we're concentrating on tracking it. We need to transfer you to a Royal Navy chopper, and for that, you're going to have to put on a survival suit."

"Why do I need a survival suit?" Harvey asked.

"It will keep you warm in the water," said Chris.

"I'm going in the water?" Harvey was so focussed on what he was doing, he wasn't able to fully grasp the significance of what Chris was saying.

"To transfer you to the navy chopper, we have to get you into a life raft," Chris explained. "But we can't hover directly over the empty raft, or the downwash from our rotor will flip it over. We're going to winch you down to the water in the rescue basket, and then Hester will swim you over to the raft."

"But my controller and goggles aren't waterproof," said Harvey, "only water-resistant."

"The rescue basket has a float at each end, so it stays at the surface. You should be fine. Make sure you keep your head and hands above the water," said Chris.

"Will do." A thought crossed Harvey's mind. "Don't I need a parental permission form for this?" he asked, half-joking but also concerned that his parents might not approve.

"No form needed, Harvey. I've been on the phone with your dad and it was his idea. He said you're a good swimmer and have a level head. So, before we continue, I need to confirm that you are comfortable with this plan. No one is going to force you to do this. It's up to you. Are we good to go?"

"I've been lowered from a chopper before," said Harvey, "only the last time it wasn't at night, it wasn't into the sea, and I wasn't weak from food poisoning. But I'm sure I'll be fine."

"You've done this before?" said Chris. "When did that happen?"

"It was back in July. The navy flew me home from school to thank me for rescuing one of their sailors, who had fallen into the sea."

"I would love to hear the rest of that story sometime," said Chris.

Harvey could hear Simon on the radio again. "Rescue one-oh-five to NPAS four-five, maintain speed of ten kilometres per hour and distance of fifty metres to starboard."

"Roger that," came the response from National Police Air Service four-five.

"NPAS four-five is the police chopper, Harvey," said Chris. "They're now flying on our starboard side and will keep an eye out for you when you're in the raft. They'll make sure you don't run into anything when we leave."

Harvey was well aware that he would be floating alone in one of the busiest shipping channels in the world. "Don't you mean they'll make sure nothing runs into *me*?" he said.

"I suppose you could put it that way," agreed Chris. "Let Hester know when you're ready for the suit."

"I'll be ready in just a second," said Harvey, "as soon as the drone is back on the water." Harvey landed the drone again and waited for the sub to come into view. "I'm ready now," he said.

"Alright, let's start by taking off your shoes," said Hester. "Could you raise your feet for me?" Harvey raised both his feet and Hester removed his shoes. "Now you need to pass me the controller."

Harvey passed the controller to Hester, and she set it down on a seat.

"Okay, so far so good. Now take two steps forward and sit down on the suit." Hester held Harvey by the arm while he took two steps forward and sat down on the open survival suit. Hester then helped him pull the suit over his legs and assisted him to a standing position before pulling the suit over his arms and zipping it up at the front.

The suit covered Harvey's feet but not his hands. With his hands free, he could still operate the drone.

Hester passed the controller back to him and then tightened the Velcro straps around his wrists. "There," she said. "That should keep the water out."

Harvey completed another hop with the drone while Hester put fins on her feet and pulled the rescue basket into position on the floor. She attached the winch cable to the basket and to her harness. "Let me know when you're ready to get into the basket, Harvey."

"I'm ready now."

"Okay, pass me the controller again. Now turn to your right. I'm going to place your hands on the side of the basket. But don't lose track of that sub."

Harvey felt the side of the basket with his hands.

"Alright, now I want you to bend over and step into the basket."

Harvey stepped into the basket and sat down. It was the same sitting position he had been in while riding in the cargo bike box.

Hester passed him back the controller. "Now I need to take the headset back," she said. "You won't be able to use it to communicate with the police or navy, and that set isn't waterproof."

"It was a pleasure having you aboard today," said Simon before Hester eased the headset off of Harvey's head.

"Passenger is in the basket," announced Hester. "Are you ready, Harvey?" she called out as she swung herself out over the side of the chopper.

Harvey wasn't sure if he would ever be completely ready. He knew that dangling mid-air in a basket with drone goggles on was going to be a strange experience. The fact that it would give him years of bragging rights crossed his mind. "Ready," he smiled.

"Release the raft," said Hester.

Alf, the other winchman, pressed a button for the raft to drop, and Simon flew the chopper far enough away so the downwash wouldn't flip the raft.

Hester watched as the raft landed on the water and self-inflated. "Raft is ready," she said. "Lower the winch."

Alf reached up and gripped the winch controller. The basket lifted slightly off the floor, and with a small push from Alf, Harvey swung feet first out the door of the chopper.

Harvey could feel himself dangling freely in mid-air. He felt himself being lowered down to the water. The motion of the basket swinging about made him thankful he hadn't eaten for a long time. This would not be a good time to start heaving his guts out.

The metal basket landed in the sea and submerged below the surface. Only the two orange floats prevented it from sinking completely. Harvey felt the water come up around him, but he was careful to keep his hands high and dry.

Hester, aided by the fins on her feet, took only a minute to push the basket over to the raft. "Harvey," she called out breathlessly when they arrived. "Pass me your controller and goggles, and I'll place them in the raft. You're going to need your hands and eyes for the next step."

Harvey passed the controller to Hester, who placed it in the raft. With his hands now free, he took off his goggles and, for the first time since he left home, could see his surroundings. The spotlights from both helicopters lit up the scene, and the spray from the downwash stung his eyes.

Hester was in front of him, smiling. "This isn't something you get to experience every day, is it?" she said as she took the goggles back from Harvey.

"It's certainly not what I expected when I woke up at three this morning."

"You're going to have quite the story to tell. Now, let's get you into the raft. You need to roll to the side to get out of the basket, and then once you're in the water you can step on my hands and I'll give you a boost up."

Harvey followed her instructions. A moment later, he was sitting comfortably with his back against the side of the raft, goggles on and controller in hand.

"I don't see the sub at the moment. Hang on a sec, I need to complete another hop to catch up with it." He flew the drone ahead another thirty metres and landed on the water. "It's still there," he said. "Same speed, same heading. We're good to go."

"That's great," said Hester. "Nice work tonight, Harvey. It was a pleasure to work with you. I have to go now before my crew decides to leave without me. The navy will be here in about twelve minutes, but don't forget, the police chopper will be watching over you the whole time."

"Thanks for the lift," Harvey replied.

Hester reached over and patted him on the back. "You'll be just fine, Harvey. Take care now." She signalled up to Alf in the chopper and then swam away from the raft before being pulled up to join her crew.

By now the sub had passed out of the view of the sonar display, and for a moment Harvey needed to focus on flying the drone again. He landed the drone once more, and the sub appeared in view.

While the drone floated on the water, Harvey reflected on his situation. It was now 4:38 a.m., and he was flying a drone with FPV goggles on while drifting alone in the English Channel in an inflatable raft. There was a submarine underneath him and a police helicopter in the air somewhere above him. It had been just over an hour and a half since he had been sleeping in his warm bed, and eight hours since he had had anything to eat. He remembered something his grandfather would often say: *Harvey, the truth is often stranger than fiction*. He wondered if any of his friends would believe him when he told them his story.

Chapter 27

THE WILDCAT

While Harvey floated alone in the raft, he checked his battery levels. The controller was still at eighty percent and would be good for a few more hours, but the battery level on the drone would probably only last another thirty minutes. This presented a challenge. In thirty minutes, he would be in the navy helicopter. How was he going to be able to change the battery from the air? The downwash from the rotors would blow the drone out of control if the chopper and the drone got too close to each other. He realised there was only one solution. He would have to change the battery now.

Harvey flew the drone back to the raft and landed it on the water, close enough that he could reach it by leaning over the side. Removing his goggles, he took a couple of seconds to look around. The spotlight from the police chopper was still on the raft. Beyond the reach of the spotlight, he could see only darkness except for distant lights on the shore. Near the entrance to Weymouth Harbour, there were numerous blue flashing lights. *There must be a dozen police cars there,* Harvey thought, *and they're all counting on me to track the sub.*

Harvey reached over the side of the raft and pulled the drone out of the water. After setting it on the floor, he unzipped the survival suit and reached into his pocket for the spare battery. With the fresh battery installed and the cover snapped shut, he set the drone back in the water, placed the flat battery on the floor of the raft, and replaced his goggles.

A moment later, the drone was in the air again and on its way back to find the submarine. By the time the drone returned to its original location, nearly three minutes had passed. Harvey did some quick maths in his head. The sub would travel one kilometre every six minutes at ten kilometres per hour, so half of that would be five hundred metres. He flew the drone back to a point roughly 550 metres ahead of the sub's last known location and waited. If the sub had changed its heading, then all would be lost.

Several tense seconds passed until the sub finally appeared on the display. Harvey's calculations had been correct. He would have to tell his maths teacher that the stuff he was teaching them actually worked in the real world.

* * *

The sound of a second chopper approaching announced the arrival of the Royal Navy. It didn't take long before Harvey heard some splashing and a voice calling him from the water next to the raft.

"Harvey, Petty Officer Emmett Shilton here to assist you," said the voice. "Are you still tracking that sub for us?"

"Yes," Harvey called back. "And I just changed the drone's battery, so I'm good to go for another ninety minutes."

"You gave us a bit of a scare when you did that," Emmett replied. "We've been communicating with the police chopper, and they saw you bring the drone back to the raft. There was concern your battery was dying. Good job thinking ahead and bringing a spare. Now, let's get you into the basket and up to our Wildcat."

Harvey removed the goggles and set them on the floor of the raft with the controller. Climbing out of the raft was a lot easier than climbing in. When Emmett saw that Harvey was sitting upright in the basket, he passed him the goggles and controller, then pushed the basket away from the raft.

A moment later there was a bit of a jerk, and once again Harvey could feel himself swaying in a metal cage as he floated mid-air beneath a helicopter while wearing FPV goggles. The basket was raised up to the Wildcat and pulled through the open door by the winchman. Emmett pulled the door shut and assisted Harvey with getting out of the basket and into his seat. Once Harvey was seated, Emmett placed a headset on him.

"Welcome aboard, Harvey," said a familiar voice on the headset. "This is Lieutenant Nate Clemence. It looks like we get to meet again. I understand your drone controller needs a little assistance extending its range?"

It was reassuring for Harvey to hear a familiar voice. Lieutenant Nate Clemence was the navy pilot who had given him a ride home from school back in July.

"Hello, Lieutenant Nate," Harvey answered. "It's good to meet you again too. My controller only has a range of six kilometres in ideal conditions, so your help is appreciated."

"You're more than welcome. I hope you realise that you're mighty fortunate to have three helicopters to help you play your little game."

Harvey laughed. "No, you're lucky to have a fish-finding drone to help you play *your* game."

There were a few chuckles before another voice said, "He really put you in your place, Nate."

"That's my co-pilot, Clay Banks," Nate explained. "You've already met our most excellent rescue swimmer, Emmett Shilton. Your winchman for today is Petty Officer Corbin Pickford. Before we get down to business, I want to know–how are you holding up? You've had quite the night, and I'm sure the food poisoning didn't help. Do you need any water? Maybe something to eat?"

"I think there's enough adrenaline coursing through my veins to keep me going for a while, but I could use some water."

"I'm glad you're in good spirits. Corbin, pass our young drone pilot some water, would you?" Nate requested. "We don't want him getting dehydrated."

Harvey could feel Corbin press a bottle against the back of his hand.

"Help yourself," Corbin said. "There's plenty more where that came from."

Harvey took a long, refreshing drink. He couldn't remember the last time water had tasted so good. He would've drunk more, but it occurred to him that going to the toilet would pose a bit of a challenge. Unlike the coach they had travelled in to London on a few days ago, there probably wasn't a toilet in the chopper, and even if there was, it would be a big challenge to take off the survival suit.

Harvey's thoughts were interrupted by the voice of Clay. "Harvey, we've been on the phone with your dad. There's a man called Carter Rhodes who owns a charter fishing business, and he owes you a favour. Your dad said you helped him out with his business by introducing him to drone fishing."

"That's right," Harvey responded. "Mr Rhodes owns Carter's Charters. He has a boat called the *Sidon*."

"That's great," said Chris. "You'll be happy to know that your dad, your brother, and Mr Carter will be joining us in the *Sidon* to provide some support. I expect your dad wants to keep a closer eye on his son. We're expecting them to catch up with us in about thirty minutes."

"The *Sidon* has some of the latest fish-finding equipment. They'll be able to help us track the sub."

"Well, it certainly can't hurt to have an extra set of eyes," Clay added.

"Do you have a plan to capture the sub yet?" Harvey asked.

"No," said Clay. "We're working on some ideas. There are half a dozen ways we could destroy it, but the Queen would not be amused if we did that. Capturing it intact is a different story."

Harvey recalled the article he'd read in *Funk and Wagnalls* about whales getting stuck in fishing nets. "Would a fishing net work?" he asked.

"It would have to be a large one," said Clay.

"Pair trawlers sometimes capture humpbacks in their nets by mistake, and humpbacks weigh as much as thirty-six thousand kilos. The submarine we're chasing only weighs about eleven thousand. There are often fishing boats returning to Weymouth in the early morning. I bet you could drum one up on the radio and get them to help."

"Good job thinking outside the box, Harvey," Nate interjected. "I think that just might work. We'll see if there are any boats in the area."

Harvey continued focussing on the task at hand while Clay and Nate worked on locating some fishing boats.

Clay's voice came back over the headset after about five minutes. "Your hunch was right, Harvey. We've located two fishing boats returning to Weymouth that are equipped with a pair trawling net. Now the challenge is going to be catching the submarine in the net. The Spiggen Class II sub was built to play Hide and Seek. It would hide, and then the Swedish Navy would try to find it as part of their training exercises. It's small, but it's sophisticated, and it would be equipped with both active and passive sonar. It's quite possible that not all the systems on the Spiggen work. It's also likely that no one in the sub knows how to operate the equipment to its full potential."

"Do you think they'll be able to detect my drone?" Harvey asked.

"They may not hear your drone's sonar signal, or they may think it's a glitch in their system and they're choosing to ignore it. So instead of us deploying *our* sonar system, we'll try to be as quiet as possible, and you keep the glitch going so we don't risk drawing their attention."

"But won't they hear the trawlers approaching?"

"They certainly will, and therein lies our dilemma. We can't get anywhere near the sub without them hearing us, and we can't capture it without getting near it. We have eight sonobuoys on this Wildcat. A sonobuoy is a sonar device attached to a buoy that we can drop anywhere in the water. We also have a more powerful dipping sonar attached to a cable. We could easily locate the sub in thirty seconds and destroy it thirty seconds later. Obviously, it would make no sense to do that. We don't have the death penalty for armed robbery in this country, and recovering the jewels from the bottom of the channel could pose a significant challenge. Unfortunately, our training didn't cover capturing submarines with giant fishing nets. We're flying by the seat of our pants on this one. Any suggestions?"

"If they're only listening to sounds in front of them, could the trawlers sneak up from behind?" Harvey asked.

"There's a chance the crew of the Spiggen aren't watching their backs, but the trawlers wouldn't be able to tow the net fast enough to catch up with the sub from the rear," Nate explained.

"What about the *Sidon*? Won't they hear it?"

"They will, but Carter's going to keep the *Sidon* about two kilometres away for the time being. We need to stay as quiet as possible until we sort this out."

Harvey thought for a moment about the problem at hand. It crossed his mind how noisy Sally was, and what a good thing it was she hadn't come with him. With the racket she made, the robbers would have easily been able to hear her when they were in the raft. He smiled to himself as he remembered her dance with the rain stick at breakfast on the day of the trip to London. Then he remembered how he was startled when his mother appeared beside him. He hadn't heard her coming because of the background noise. And then, suddenly, Harvey had an epiphany.

"What if," Harvey wondered aloud, "we made so much noise they couldn't hear the trawlers approaching? What if you deployed your entire sonar system in the water in active mode at the same time as the *Sidon* did, and the trawlers approached and started circling the sub at full throttle? With the two trawlers, the *Sidon*, your dipper, and eight sonobuoys, that would be twelve different sources of sound. They might not be able to figure out what was going on."

"Young man, you are a genius," Nate laughed. "That was a nuclear-powered brain wave. And make that thirteen sources of sound. There's a police boat on the way, too." He paused. "I'm curious, Harvey. What made you think of that brilliant idea?"

"It was my sister, Sally. She's so noisy sometimes you can barely think, let alone hear what's going on around you."

"You'll have to thank her for us when you see her. Now, I have an idea. An interagency operation like this needs a code name. Are you okay if we call it Operation Sally?"

"Sounds good to me," Harvey grinned.

"Perfect, we'll go with that. When Operation Sally commences, the sonar display in the sub will light up like a Christmas tree. Most likely, they'll assume it's malfunctioned and come to a stop while they attempt to figure out what's going on."

"What about my drone's fish finder? Will I still be able to track the sub with all the noise?"

"You'll be fine," Nate assured him. "You're looking straight down with that fish finder, and the noise will be coming from the sides."

Chapter 28

CATCH OF THE DAY

It had been almost an hour since the sub dove under the water in Weymouth Bay, and ten minutes since Harvey had the brainwave to overwhelm the sub's sonar systems with too much noise. In that time, Harvey continued to keep up his sub-tracking. His lack of food over the past couple of days was starting to take a toll on his body, and he was becoming more tired by the minute, but thankfully the adrenaline continued to do its job. He wondered if his life would ever be this exciting again, or whether the rest of it would seem dull in comparison.

Nate's voice interrupted Harvey's thoughts. "Operation Sally is about to swing into action. We've got the two trawlers on track to intercept the sub at exactly oh-five-hundred hours. The call sign for the police boat is Flare Niner-Two-Five, and it will arrive from the north side, and the *Sidon* will come in from the south side at the same time. They'll both start circling the sub at full throttle, and the *Sidon* will activate its side-imaging sonar at the same time we deploy our sonobuoys. Once those are in the water, we'll place them into active mode. Harvey, we need you to keep tracking with the drone. The only way any of us are going to know the sub's location is by watching the blinking light on the drone. I need you to take shorter and more frequent hops, so you're always as close to the sub as possible. It will also make it easier for the boats to see the drone's lights if you aren't on the surface as long."

"Roger that," Harvey replied. "Do you think it's going to work?"

"It had better work," Nate answered, "or we'll be heading into an all-night game of cat and mouse, and we don't have enough fuel for that. Fortunately, there are already three more sonar-equipped navy choppers waiting to take over from us if our fuel runs low. Plus, there's a navy frigate preparing to launch in the morning. We've also got the French Navy on alert in case the sub heads their way, and a US aircraft carrier on training exercises has offered to help."

"Wow," said Harvey. "This is a huge deal, isn't it?"

"Yes, sir. It looks like you may have thwarted the single largest robbery in the history of the world. I suppose you could call it a big deal, but don't let it go to your head. We're about to go live with the plan, and we need you focussed on the task at hand. No more unnecessary chit chat. Could you confirm the heading and depth of the target?"

"Heading 102 degrees," said Harvey. "Depth holding at twenty metres."

There was a pause, then Nate said, "Flare Niner-Two-Five, *Sidon* and trawlers have confirmed visual on the drone. Trawlers have confirmed net is ready. Trawlers at three hundred metres. Corbin, launch first sonobuoy and one every two seconds."

Corbin, who was sitting in front of an array of controls and screens, pressed some buttons. Under the chopper, the first sonobuoy canister was jettisoned from the helicopter and fell into the water below. Nate was flying a circular path around the rear of the sub's location, so the sonobuoys were dropped in a similar arcing pattern. As the sonobuoys landed in the water, their canisters opened up with the buoy portion floating to the surface and the sonar portion suspended below by a cable that joined the two components together. Signals from the sonar were sent up the cable to an antenna on the buoy, and from there, wirelessly transmitted to the chopper.

"Trawlers are now at two hundred metres. Corbin, we'll wait to see what happens before dropping the dipping sonar. Deploying it now will restrict our mobility, and there's a good chance we won't need it."

"Roger. Sonobuoys in the water and ready to go," confirmed Corbin.

"Wildcat to *Sidon*," said Nate. "Activate side sonar. Commence full throttle circling of sub. Use drone as centre point."

On board the *Sidon*, Carter activated his side sonar and opened up the throttle.

"Wildcat to Flare Niner-Two-Five, commence circling target," Nate instructed. "Match speed of *Sidon*. Corbin, activate sonobuoys. Let's light up their sonar display and see what they do. Harvey, report any changes in the sub's speed, heading or depth."

Harvey noticed that with his latest hop, his drone had landed in the water well ahead of the submarine.

"Sub appears to be slowing," Harvey reported excitedly.

"Confirmed," said Corbin. "I have eyes on the sub now, too. It's stopped completely."

There was a tense moment waiting to see what would happen. Harvey tried to imagine what the sub operators were thinking. Were they wondering if their equipment had failed, or did they suspect they were sur-rounded?

"Harvey, are you seeing what I'm seeing?" Corbin asked. "The sub appears to be surfacing."

"It *is* surfacing," Harvey confirmed. "And they're right under me, so I'm taking off. I don't want the sub to tip over my drone." Harvey flew the drone up into the air above the sub's location. If the drone were to tip over, he would no longer be able to participate in Operation Sally, and this was likely the single most exciting thing he had ever done in his entire life.

"Harvey, maintain altitude of ten metres," said Nate. "We still need your eyes down there."

"Roger that," said Harvey.

"All units be advised, target is surfacing," said Nate.

Floodlights from the police boat and helicopters lit up the area just before the nose of the sub broke the sur-face. The sub immediately levelled off with a splash. Eve-ryone waited in agonising silence to see what would hap-pen next.

Finally, the hatch on the sub's conning tower popped open. A man stuck his head out and glanced around. He seemed surprised. The police boat moved in closer. Har-vey could see the officer on the boat was shouting into a megaphone.

The man's head disappeared from the conning tower for a moment and then reappeared. This time he held a machine gun in his hands. Harvey could see him aim the gun at the police boat and start shooting. Both police officers on the boat dived behind the steering console of their rigid hull inflatable boat. The police were pinned down and the flood light was dropped. The man shot again. It didn't look like the steering console was strong enough to withstand many bullets.

Without hesitating, Harvey did the one thing he could do: he aimed the drone straight at the man and opened the throttle. The drone smashed into the man's right arm with enough force to knock the gun out of his hands. The weapon hit the deck of the submarine before sliding into the water. With two broken booms, the drone bounced off the man's arm and followed the gun into the sea.

"Well done, Harvey!" cheered Nate.

"Thanks," Harvey grinned. "I didn't know what else to do!"

"You did the right thing by sacrificing your drone. That was some quick thinking. You've just made a couple of new friends."

"Is their boat going to sink now? It looked like one of the inflatable tubes was deflating."

"Don't you worry about that. Any respectable RIB is designed to float with both tubes deflated. As you probably know the 'R' in RIB stands for 'Rigid'. The rigid portion will float on its own. The inflatable tubes are there for extra buoyancy. On a calm sea like this one they'll be fine."

"Glad to hear it," Harvey replied.

It didn't concern him that he had just lost his most valuable drone. It seemed insignificant compared to the fact that he had likely just saved two lives. Secretly he'd hoped the police officers would need to be rescued by the helicopter so he could meet his new friends.

Harvey removed his goggles and was setting them on the seat beside him when Nate said, "He's closed the hatch. It looks like they're preparing to dive again."

Harvey stood up to look out the window and watched as the sub disappeared beneath the water. "Perfect," said Nate. "They're heading straight toward the gap between the trawlers."

"You're right," Corbin agreed. "They're maintaining a heading of 102 degrees and headed straight for the trawling net. They're in for a surprise in about ten seconds."

Harvey counted down the seconds in his head as he watched the two trawlers getting closer.

Just as Harvey got to nought, Corbin said, "Sub has stopped. Sub is in the net and is being pulled backwards by the trawlers."

A cheer went up inside the chopper and a wave of relief swept through Harvey's body.

Chapter 29

HOMEWARD BOUND

In spite of the sub having been captured, the excitement was far from over. Harvey continued watching out the window of the Wildcat as the two trawlers passed beneath it. He turned to his right to look down at the *Sidon* and spotted Jack waving up at the chopper. He waved back, but he doubted Jack could see him. His dad appeared to be on the phone. Harvey wondered who he was speaking to. The answer came almost immediately.

"Harvey, I'm on the phone with your dad," said Nate. "He said it's your bedtime. He wants you winched down so they can take you home. You think you're up for another basket ride?"

"I'm completely knackered. But another basket ride will be fine."

"It was a pleasure to have you aboard, young man. I hope we meet again sometime."

Emmett took off Harvey's headset and helped him climb back into the basket. He then double-checked that the basket was securely attached to the winch, fastened his own harness, opened the door, and swung himself out. Corbin pushed Harvey, head first, after Emmett. For the third time that night, Harvey dangled in a basket at the end of a winch cable, only this time he could see everything that was happening.

The navigation light was the first thing that appeared in view as Harvey was lowered down to the *Sidon's* deck. The light was followed by the sight of his dad's smiling face. Standing beside his dad was Jack, giving two thumbs up. Mr Ranger held one side of the basket, and with Emmett still holding the other side, both men guided it to the deck. The basket touched down with a gentle bump. Radar, who had also come along for the ride, placed his front paws on the side and licked Harvey's face. Jack reached down and grabbed Harvey under one arm and helped pull him to his feet.

Now standing, the exhausted hero turned and stepped into his father's arms. The stress and excitement of the last couple of hours was over. There was no longer a need for his body to be in fight or flight mode. With the adrenaline pump shut off, he felt a wave of emotion sweep through him that left him sobbing and not really understanding why.

"It's okay, Harvey," said Mr Ranger as he continued to hold his youngest son. "You've done a great job tonight, and you've been through a lot. It doesn't help that you're weak from lack of food. You're safe now. Just let it out."

"We're so proud of you," Jack added. "You were brilliant. That bloke with the gun had no idea what hit him."

"Thanks, Jack." Harvey took a couple of deep breaths.

"He's been a real trooper!" said Emmett. "Now go get some sleep, Harvey, and you'll feel much better." He turned and signalled to the chopper before being winched back up to the Wildcat, taking the basket with him.

Mr Ranger was still holding Harvey when Harvey pointed to the starboard side of the boat.

"Look, what's Radar up to?" Harvey said. Radar was standing on the gunwale, staring into the water. He was crouching, ready to jump.

"Radar, stop!" Jack yelled. It was too late. Radar had jumped into the water. Jack rushed to look over the side to see what Radar was doing. Radar was already swimming back to the boat with something in his mouth. "Look, Harvey. He's got your drone!"

Carter opened up a small gate on the side of the *Sidon*, allowing Jack to easily reach down and pull Radar back aboard. "Well done, boy," Jack praised. "You've saved some valuable evidence."

"There's no evidence," Harvey groaned. "I forgot to press the record button. But great job getting my drone back, Radar. Hopefully I'll be able to fix it with some spare parts."

Carter closed the gate and returned to the wheelhouse where he opened the throttle and headed the *Sidon* for home. Jack picked up a backpack from the deck. "Mum sent you a snack," he said to his brother, pulling out a lunch bag. "She said you still need to take it easy or you're gonna feel awful again."

"*Awful* is a good thing, meaning *full of awe*," Harvey quipped. "I think Mum meant to say that my stomach would feel horrible."

Jack turned and looked at their father. "He's acting normal, Dad. I think that's a good sign."

"It certainly is," Mr Ranger chuckled as he headed toward the wheelhouse to speak with Carter.

A moment later, he returned. "Weymouth Harbour will be swarming with the media by now. They'll want to know why there's been so much hubbub over Weymouth this morning, and why a small army of police officers has been searching along the shore."

"So what are we going to do, Dad?" Harvey asked.

"Instead of pulling into Weymouth Harbour, Carter is going to drop us off at Newton's Cove. Jack will go and retrieve the cargo bike from Carter's house. Do you think you'll be okay climbing a few steps, Harvey?"

"I'll be fine," said Harvey as he finished a banana and started to munch on a piece of cold toast.

The return trip in the *Sidon* was uneventful. It didn't take long for Jack to retrieve the cargo bike and deliver Harvey to their home. After dropping off his electronics at RISC, Harvey, with Jack's assistance, removed the survival suit and then both boys crashed into their beds.

For several minutes, Harvey lay awake contemplating the events of the past few hours. When at last he was about to fall asleep, he heard Sally clomping down the stairs. He knew that Sally had almost certainly slept through all the noise of the previous evening and therefore woken up at her usual 6:30 a.m. He figured that once she realised everyone else was still sleeping, she would take it upon herself to make breakfast. And in Sally's seven-year-old mind, every meal should be a party with fancy decorations.

Harvey smiled as he heard his sister opening and closing cupboard doors. He imagined her covering the dining table with the red tablecloth that was typically used for Christmas and Thanksgiving. No doubt she would massacre some plants from the garden and use them to make a centrepiece.

"Hey Jack," Harvey whispered. "Are you still awake?"

"Yeah. What is it?"

"We're in for a feast when we get up."

"I heard that too. Sal's going to have a heyday down there."

After a minute, Harvey spoke again. "Jack, I've just thought of something else."

"What is it now? I need to go to sleep."

"I left my shoes in the Coast Guard chopper."

Don't worry about it. That survival suit is worth more than ten pairs of shoes. They're going to want to do a trade at some point. Now go to sleep."

Chapter 30

BREAKFAST CELEBRATION

At 9:45 a.m., Harvey, and quite possibly everyone else that was still sleeping within a five-hundred-metre radius, was awakened by the ringing of a loud bell. It was a rather piercing and violent type of ringing that can only come from a large dinner bell in the hands of an excited seven-year-old. The ringing was followed by Sally yelling, "Breakfast, breakfast. I made breakfast for everyone. Come and get your lovely breeeeaaakfast!"

Harvey lay motionless for a few minutes. His eyes were still closed when hurricane Sally swept into his room and jumped on his bed, ringing the bell again.

"Come on, Harvey! I've made the best breakfast ever. You're going to love it."

Harvey would have preferred to lie there for a while, but previous experience had taught him that trying to do so would be futile. He pulled himself out of bed as soon as Sally started to attack Jack. A short pillow fight ensued, during which Harvey and Jack had to show considerable restraint and from which Sally emerged the clear winner.

When Harvey, Jack, and Sally arrived in the dining room, their parents were already there waiting for them. It was Saturday, and everyone except Harvey was in their pyjamas. Wearing pyjamas for breakfast on Saturday was a bit of a tradition in the Ranger household. "It's not like the queen or the prime minister is just going to show up on a Saturday," Mrs Ranger would say. Jack would always reply with, "It's not like the queen or the prime minister is going to show up for breakfast any day." Then Harvey would say, "I don't know why you even bother with pyjamas."

Harvey surveyed the room. Most of his predictions about what Sally had been up to proved to be correct, but this Saturday she'd had more time than usual and had really outdone herself. Harvey noticed there were name tags telling everyone where to sit. *That's a nice touch,* he thought. *Just in case I forget where I've been sitting for the past eleven years.* There were balloons of all different colours taped to the walls around the room, and twirly paper things hung down from the mantelpiece. It was indeed a sight to behold.

"Sally," said Mrs Ranger, "this meal looks truly scrumptious. It's a masterpiece. You've done such an amazing job."

The others all agreed, but Harvey knew his mum was probably groaning on the inside at the thought of all the clean-up that would be required.

"What are we celebrating this time?" asked Jack. Sally's frequent need to have a party usually meant stretching the limits on what would often be considered party-worthy, and her justifications were a source of amusement.

"We're celebrating our family," said Sally. "I love my mummy, my daddy, my big brother and my not-so-big brother, and I want to celebrate." There wasn't a single person in the room who could object to that.

"We've got something else to celebrate," said Mr Ranger. He went on to tell Sally about everything that had happened the night before.

"Wow, what an epic adventure. Harvey, you're going to be world famous! Aren't you glad I made a nice fancy breakfast for you?" said Sally.

"Thanks, Sal," said Harvey. "I'm ravenous, but before we eat can someone check the news on their phone? I can't wait to find out what happened after we went to bed."

Jack pulled out his mobile phone and looked at Mrs Ranger questioningly. In the Ranger home, electronic devices were not allowed at the table.

"Go ahead," said Mrs Ranger. "This is an exceptional circumstance." The truth is that she was dying to know too.

"The headline says *Most Crown Jewels Recovered!*" read Jack. "Harvey, well done! Let see what else it says:

Thanks to a tip from an anonymous member of the public, a small submarine being used to smuggle the Crown Jewels out of the country was captured early this morning in the English Channel. Most of the jewels appear to have been recovered, except for the centrepiece of the entire collection, St Edward's Crown.

The capture of the submarine was a result of a large joint force operation that has been dubbed *Operation Sally*. Operation Sally involved the Coast Guard, Dorset Police, Royal Navy, some local fishermen, and an independent security expert.

Police aren't saying who the security expert is or how they helped. It is believed that this individual may have connections within MI5, but police spokespersons are neither confirming nor denying this possibility. The police did tell us that without this expert, the recovery of the Crown Jewels would not have been possible and that the security expert has been credited with saving the lives of two police officers.

Operation Sally is still ongoing today as the police attempt to round up all the robbers and recover St Edward's Crown. Also still missing is Yeoman Warder Nicholas Sparks. Police believe the gang had help from the inside and are currently working on the theory that one or more yeomen may have been involved. The hotline police setup has been overwhelmed with people calling in with tips. Police would like to remind callers to only call if they notice anything out of the ordinary that might be related to the robbery."

"Yeoman Nick was the guide for our school trip," said Harvey. "There's no way he was involved. He was so nice and friendly, and funny. I can't believe he would do something like that."

"Maybe he was taken as a hostage," said Mr Ranger. "He wasn't on the submarine, and he wasn't on the boat that delivered the jewels to the sub, so I wonder where he could be?"

"I certainly hope he's okay and that they find him," said Mrs Ranger. "And while the police are sorting this all out, let's take the opportunity to celebrate Harvey's role in the operation." Mrs Ranger turned and looked at her middle child. "It sounds like you did a super job last night, Mr Independent Security Expert."

"Yes, jolly well done, Mr Anonymous Member of the Public," said Jack, patting his brother on the back.

Mr Ranger put his arm around Harvey and said, "We're so proud of you. Now let's hope the press doesn't figure out who the independent security expert is. It's important that you *remain* an anonymous member of the public."

"I'm confused," said Sally. "Is Harvey the independent security expert or the non-mouse member of the public?"

"He's both, sweetheart," said Mr Ranger. "He's the *anonymous* member of the public, which means they don't know his name, and he's also the independent security expert. The media don't know that though, and let's hope it stays that way."

"Oh, now I understand," Sally said. "But what about Operation Sally? What's that all about? Why are they using my name to talk about an operation?"

"When different government forces or agencies work together on a joint operation, they like to give it a name," said Harvey. "Last night they decided to name it after you."

"But why me?"

"It's because you're…" Harvey paused for a second. "It's because you're special."

Sally beamed. The government had named an operation after her. She didn't fully understand what that meant, but it sounded exciting and now it was time for some wonderful food. "Okay everyone, please be seated, and I will bring you the apple teasers."

Sally started towards the kitchen but stopped in the doorway. "By the way," she said, "a police officer came to our house this morning. She said something about someone phoning in a report of a whale that wasn't a whale. I told her that we were all sleeping last night so the call couldn't have come from our house. She apologised and said that she must have the wrong address."

"Thanks for letting us know Sally," said Mr Ranger. "Normally I would follow up with the police, but this time we'll let it go."

* * *

Sally returned a minute later and announced, "Here are the apple teasers!"

The Ranger family admired the plate of mystery treats, which turned out to be large slices of apple topped with slabs of chocolate and a dollop of whipped cream.

They ate their apple teasers with comments of "delicious" and "mmm" and "where did you get the recipe?"

Sally went back to the kitchen for more.

"These are the horse doovers," she said as she walked back into the dining room carrying a wide tray.

The supposed hors d'oeuvres had so much whipped cream on them, it was difficult for anyone to tell what was underneath.

"Don't they look lovely?" Sally beamed.

The family all made an effort to look impressed and consumed the hors d'oeuvres with vigour to show their appreciation, because they knew how much it meant to Sally. Harvey was still feeling ravenous. He downed mouthful after mouthful of the delicious treats, until a little voice inside his head started telling him that perhaps it was time to slow down.

Once again Sally headed for the kitchen, and once again she returned with her arms full. "This is dessert," she declared. She carried a platter of waffles topped with strawberries and more whipped cream. On top of the whipped cream were rainbow coloured sprinkles and chocolate chips.

Everyone smiled and said politely, "Just one please," except for Harvey, who declined by saying, "I feel like I've already eaten about ten desserts."

It wasn't long before everyone had eaten as much whipped cream as they could handle. Sally carried the tray of leftovers back to the kitchen. Mr and Mrs Ranger went upstairs to get dressed in their usual Saturday attire. Jack followed them with his beloved pet and headed for the tub, where he was going to give Radar a bath, and Harvey went to lie down on the sofa.

Chapter 31

THE VISITOR

For a few moments, life in the Ranger household was quiet and relatively normal. Harvey lay on the sofa with a gradually increasing awareness that he had enjoyed Sally's breakfast a little too much, but still feeling well enough to enjoy moments of quiet that were interrupted only occasionally by a crash from the kitchen.

The relative quiet didn't last long. Sally appeared in the room carrying paper and markers, apparently having forgotten about cleaning up the dining room and kitchen. She set the markers and paper down on the coffee table.

Harvey watched his sister with curiosity. She taped four sheets of paper together to make a banner and proceeded to write *Sally's Sublime Slime Shop* in large pink letters. Harvey watched her go into the front hall and tape the banner to the side of the storage bench. Then she retrieved a box from her room containing her entire slime collection. She arranged the slime collection neatly on top of the bench. It was time to do business, it seemed.

"Who wants to buy some slime?" Sally called out at the top of her voice. "Come and get some slime. Lovely, stretchy, colourful slime. Come and get it while it's still sliiiiimy!"

Harvey covered his ears.

Sally's jingle had just finished echoing off the walls when the doorbell rang. Impressed with the promptness and effectiveness of her impromptu marketing campaign, she rushed to open the door. She was sure this must be someone who had come to buy some slime.

A large man with a very bald head stood in the doorway. Behind the man was a large black car and two motorcycles in the driveway. Blocking the driveway were three SUVs, and standing outside the SUVs were some very official looking people, all wearing dark suits. One of the women carried a large gun. The man who had rung the bell looked down at Sally and smiled.

Before he could speak, Sally asked, "Are you here to buy some slime?"

"No thank you," said the bald-headed man. "We're here for Mr Harvey Ranger." He turned and gestured towards the driveway. "The Prime Minister's in the car, and she would like to have a word with Mr Harvey, if that's okay with your parents."

"Umm yes, I'll check," Sally said, feeling puzzled by the situation as well as disappointed that the man clearly wasn't there to buy some slime. Sally turned and shouted upstairs, "Mum, Dad, the prime minister is here to see Harvey. Can she come in?"

Assuming Sally was just playing a game, Mr Ranger decided to play along. "Yes, Sally, please let the prime minister in. Show her into the living room, and tell her Harvey isn't contagious. Maybe you could offer her one of your hors d'oeuvres."

Sally turned back to the man and said, "Yes, she can come in. Harvey's in the living room, and he isn't contagious."

The bald man thanked her and went back to the car. He opened the rear door, and out stepped none other than Prime Minister Kim Wilberforce. The man walked with her to the front door and introduced her to Sally. "Sally, this is Prime Minister Kim Wilberforce and Prime Minister, this is Miss Sally Ranger."

Sally couldn't believe that the prime minister was about to enter her home, and she wondered why her parents weren't coming down the stairs to greet her. She would just have to manage the situation herself. Bowing to the prime minister, she said in her most formal and polite voice, "Your Majesty, please come this way. Harvey is in the living room. He's very tired from his epic adventure and just getting over a hot dog, but don't worry, he isn't contagious."

The prime minister smiled. "Sally," she said, "I'm not majestic. The queen is majestic. You can simply call me Prime Minister."

"Well then, Prime Minister, would you please be kind enough to follow me?" Sally led the prime minister through the hall, past Sally's Sublime Slime Shop, and into the living room where Harvey was resting on the sofa.

Harvey looked up from the sofa as they entered. He knew he wasn't feeling one hundred percent and he'd had a challenging night, but for a moment he wondered whether he was imagining things after all. Was this actually Kim Wilberforce standing in the living room in front of him?

"Harvey," said Sally, "this is the Prime Minister."

Harvey got up from the sofa and held out his hand. "Pleased to meet you, Mrs Prime Minister."

Sally corrected him, "It's just *Prime Minister*, not *Mrs Prime Minister*."

"Thank you, Sally," said the prime minister.

"You're welcome," said Sally and then she excused herself from the room before heading back to the kitchen. Sally had remembered the security people waiting around outside, and this presented a golden opportunity to share some of her kitchen creations.

Chapter 32

A DREAM FULFILLED

Harvey stood facing the prime minister in the living room.

"So you're the Harvey Ranger I've been hearing so much about?" she said.

"I suppose that's me," Harvey replied.

"I was in the area today thanking all those involved in the recovery of the Crown Jewels, and I wanted to drop by to thank you personally. From what I've been told, you're the hero from last night. You're the main character in the story, and everyone else just played a supporting role. You not only enabled us to recover the jewels, but you almost certainly saved the lives of two police officers."

"Thank you." Harvey smiled, but the smile was a little forced. The whipped cream wonders were starting to have a more significant impact on the state of peace that normally reigned in his digestive system. Harvey wasn't sure if things were going to end well.

The prime minister continued, "As you probably know by now, the submarine you spotted last night was being used to smuggle the Crown Jewels out of the country. Thanks to you, we were able to stop the thieves just in time. Unfortunately, most of the gang members, including that Smelliwig character, are still at large. Furthermore, we weren't able to recover St Edward's Crown. We believe that Smelliwig, after seeing your drone, feared the game was up. We suspect that he allowed most of the jewels to be loaded into the sub, but he took the crown from the cooler and escaped with it in the fishing boat. The fishing boat was found drifting near Weymouth Beach. It's possible Smelliwig and the other two men leapt out into the water near the beach when they saw all the flashing lights near the harbour. We have reason to believe Smelliwig is extremely dangerous. One of the reasons I wanted to thank you personally is that a public acknowledgement wouldn't be wise. It would put you in danger. This all needs to be kept very hush-hush. Do you understand, Harvey?"

Harvey nodded his head and said, "Yes, hush-hush. I understand."

Harvey hoped the prime minister would soon be finished with her speech so he could excuse himself and lie down again.

She went on, "I understand that two of your drones were damaged during your escapades. I can assure you that the government will compensate you in a way that is fitting for someone who has contributed so much to his country."

Harvey forced a smile. Sally's breakfast was not sitting well in his stomach, but he had always been taught not to interrupt. You especially try not to interrupt an adult, and when that adult is the leader of your country, the most powerful person in all the land, interrupting is absolutely not an option.

The prime minister continued speaking. Harvey heard phrases like "outstanding citizen" and "fine young man," but his thoughts lay elsewhere. He had a strong sense this meeting was not going to end well. Sally's treats were going to come back up, and it wasn't a question of if, but when. The horse doovers had already left the barn.

Kim Wilberforce had just finished saying, "What a pleasure it was to meet you," when it happened so fast that even Harvey, with all his recent experience, was caught off guard. He didn't even have time to turn away.

He vomited all over the prime minister's blouse, pants, and shoes.

Despite herself and her better judgement, the prime minister let out a small, somewhat dignified scream. "Oh dear," she said, putting aside her own immediate need. "Are you okay?" She placed her hand on Harvey's shoulder. "Why don't you lie down on the sofa again?"

Harvey, still looking pale, lay down gratefully. "I'm okay. I'm so sorry. I didn't mean to...I mean, I couldn't help it. This is so embarrassing."

★ ★ ★

Upstairs, Mr and Mrs Ranger had been finishing dressing. It was starting to get warm, so Mr Ranger went to open their bedroom window. The window faced the front of the house. Glancing out the window he was astonished to see the vehicles and security people in the driveway. Sally was standing there with a tray in her hands, passing out napkins and something covered in whipped cream to everyone.

It didn't take Mr Ranger more than two seconds to figure out who they were. Only one person travelled around England with that much security. Sally hadn't been playing around after all: the prime minister was downstairs at the very moment. "Sally wasn't fooling around," he called to his wife. "Kim Wilberforce is here! In our living room!"

Mr and Mrs Ranger hurried out of the bedroom and were just at the top of the stairs when they heard the scream. They rushed down the stairs and entered the living room just as the prime minister was about to leave the room to call them. They were followed almost immediately by the bald-headed security man, who had also heard the scream.

Mr Ranger entered the room first, "What's going on? Is everyone okay?" he said.

"I threw up," said Harvey.

"On me," added the prime minister.

"I'm so sorry!" said Mrs Ranger, "and welcome to our home." While shaking the prime minister's hand, she tried to figure out what to do next. Was there a correct protocol for cleaning vomit off a prime minister, she wondered? She decided to stall for more time. "Do you fancy a cup of tea?" she asked?

Kim Wilberforce did not immediately respond. She didn't think she wanted a cup of tea at that moment, but she wasn't sure if she should just say yes to be polite. She turned and looked at the bald-headed man, in case he might know the appropriate response for this situation. The bald-headed man was a bachelor and had never raised a child. Consequently, he had no experience cleaning up vomit, and in fact the mere thought of it struck fear deep in his soul. He raised his hands as if to say *I have no idea.*

Now, no one knows why what happened next actually happened when it did. It might have been the change in the humidity from the door being opened, or perhaps the vibrations from the footsteps of three people rushing into the room. But, whatever it was, it caused the molecular bonding between the long-forgotten slime and the ceiling to start to let go. At the moment when the force of gravity was stronger than the sticky force holding the slime to the ceiling, the slime accelerated downward, following Newton's second law, and landed with a large flopping plop on top of the bald head of the bald-headed man.

There was a moment of awkward silence, and then came a small muffled laugh from the mouth of the prime minister. She didn't mean to laugh, but she couldn't help herself. She laughed again, only this time she didn't hold anything back. The bald-headed man started to laugh next, and it was just a few seconds before everyone in the room was laughing hysterically.

When she finally caught her breath, the prime minister said, "Oh dear, what am I going to do? I can't go out in public like this."

It was at that moment that Mrs Ranger realised an opportunity to have a dream fulfilled. "I'm a wardrobe consultant," she said reassuringly. "I run a small business called The Wardrobe OR, as in *wardrobe operating room*, and I have lots of clothes in your size and for your type. Why don't you come with me, and we'll get you all sorted out?"

The prime minister didn't have any spare clothes with her that were suitable for work, so she had no choice but to go along with Mrs Ranger's suggestion. She did admire what Mrs Ranger was wearing. It was apparent to her that Mrs Ranger had a sense of style. Uncertain as to whether this would be okay with her security team, she looked questioningly at the bald-headed man.

"It's okay," he said. "Mrs Ranger has security clearance. We checked her background this morning."

"Thank you," said Mrs Ranger and then gestured towards the door. "Please, come with me."

During the next hour, Mr Ranger cleaned the carpet in the living room while Sally peddled her wares to the security team and Harvey chatted with the bald-headed man.

At one point, Harvey decided his teeth were long overdue for a brushing and headed to the bathroom upstairs. Passing his parents' bedroom door, he could hear his mother and the prime minister talking. Their conversation sounded pleasant and somewhat intense. Harvey was much too polite to stick around long enough to listen, but if he had he would have heard words like *taxation*, *debt* and *immigration* mixed in with other words and phrases, like *personality type* and *accessories* and *that doesn't quite work for you.*

Chapter 33

SAYING GOODBYE

Kim Wilberforce looked fabulous in her new outfit when she finally came down the stairs to join the others. Mrs Ranger came down behind her, beaming with pride. Her smile shrank somewhat as her daughter began to speak.

"That outfit is simply epic," Sally gushed. "You don't look frumpy at all now."

Then everyone else said how wonderful the prime minister looked, and Sally's comment was quickly forgotten. Even Harvey and Jack, who were generally lacking in awareness of such matters, thought Kim Wilberforce looked so much better now that their mum had worked her magic on her.

They all walked outside to the awaiting cars. The prime minister turned to Harvey. "I want to thank you again for your service to our country," she said. "We'll try to resolve the damaged drone situation as soon as possible."

Harvey apologised again for throwing up on her.

"Oh, don't worry about that. It will make a wonderful story for my grandchildren."

"That's true," Harvey said, "but it all has to be kept very hush-hush."

The prime minister smiled and said, "Oh yes, thanks for reminding me."

Then Sally walked up to the prime minister, handed her some bright red slime, and said, "This is for you. Remember, it will help you relax, so play with it often."

The prime minister said, "Thank you, Sally. That is by far the most wonderful slime anyone has given me. I would venture to guess that it is the most wonderful slime that anyone has given any prime minister in the history of our country."

The prime minister turned to Mrs Ranger next. "Olivia," she said, "I'll try to return the clothes as soon as possible. Actually, I would love for you to come to Number 10 to help me with my whole wardrobe sometime. I also want you to know that I thoroughly enjoyed our conversation. Even though we have different political views, you're able to carry on a respectful conversation without exaggerating or twisting the truth. I rarely enjoy a conversation as much as that. I think we could become good friends."

"It would be an honour to visit you at Number 10," Mrs Ranger smiled. "I enjoyed our conversation too."

The two women hugged each other, and then everyone else shook hands–except for Sally, who heartily hackled all the members of the security team. Then, without further ado, the whole entourage got into their vehicles and, as quickly as they had arrived, they were gone.

Harvey, now feeling quite a bit better, joined the rest of the family in the living room to discuss everything that had happened that morning.

Chapter 34

STORIES SHARED

Shortly after noon, the doorbell rang for a second time that day. Harvey opened the door to find James standing outside.

"Did you sleep in this morning?" James asked. "You missed a boatload of excitement down at the harbour. I tried calling you several times around half past eight, but you didn't answer. You must have heard they captured the jewel thieves in the bay?"

"Yeah, it was all over the news. What excitement did you see that I missed?" asked Harvey.

"The noise of the helicopters woke me up around quarter past four," James replied. "They were really loud. I grabbed my binoculars and watched for a bit through the window. There was a coast guard *and* a police chopper. They were following this small blinking red light that would land on the water and then rise slightly off the water before moving a bit to the east and landing again. It reminded me of your fishing drone, but it must have been some kind of device that was being used by the coast guard or police to track the submarine."

"That's strange. I wonder what that was?"

"Dunno, but eventually they were too far away to see what was happening, so I went back to bed. When I read the news this morning, I learned that most of the jewels had been recovered and that the prime minister had come to town and was personally congratulating everyone involved. I tried to call you and then went down to the harbour to see what was going on. As you probably heard, the thieves had tried escaping in a small submarine, and the police managed to bag them in a giant fishing net. When I got there, the fishing boats and the sub were still there blocking up the harbour and the prime minister was just leaving with her security people. I can't believe you missed all the excitement! Old Man Abott said he hadn't seen that much fuss in the harbour since D-Day. You chose a bad day to sleep in."

"Yeah. It's a real bummer that I missed it. I can't believe they caught them right here in Weymouth. It would have been great if I could have gone with you."

"What would have been really great is if *you* had been the one who spotted them with one of your drones.

Can you imagine the headlines? *Drone-Boy Stops Jewel Thieves*, or *Boy from Weymouth Thwarts Thieves in Largest Robbery in the History of the World*. You would've received a personal thank-you from the prime minister, and probably a big reward. You'd have international fame for at least a week!"

"Well, guess what? I have huge news, too. The prime minister actually did come to our house!"

"What? Why? You're yanking my chain!"

"No, seriously. She needed my mum's help with a wardrobe situation."

"Why didn't she just go to a clothing store?"

"Uhh…dunno. Didn't ask. I suppose she wanted the best and didn't want to go somewhere that was open to the public."

"Your mum must have been really excited. She's so into clothes and wardrobes and colours and all that stuff."

"She was stoked. And by the time the prime minister left, it seemed like she and my mum were becoming good friends. She said she wanted my mum to visit her at Number 10 sometime. So, what did you do for the rest of the morning?" asked Harvey, not wanting to spend too much time on the topic of the prime minister's visit.

"I ended up chatting with Carter for a while. He couldn't get his boat out of the harbour for his nine o'clock charter. There were two men with him who were supposed to go on the trip. They had driven all the way down here from Aldershot this morning and were really disappointed they couldn't go fishing. Carter didn't seem too disappointed. He just seemed tired. Anyhow, the men weren't too happy. They'd just driven two hours to go on an epic fishing adventure. So, I offered to take them out in my gramp's Zodiac. They accepted, and we launched the boat off the beach with the transom wheels."

"That's great. Did they pay you?"

"Of course. They paid me a hundred pounds for two hours of fishing and cruising along the coast. We would have gone longer, but no toilet and all that. Anyway, you would not believe it: we saw a whale!"

"Where was it? Were you in the bay?"

"Yeah. About a kilometre off the coast by Durdle Door. The whale was a bit further out. It was a genuine bonafide humpback whale. We all took pictures with our phones. *Their* pictures were rubbish, but mine were half decent, so we agreed that I would send them to the newspaper. I'm going to be famous!" James glanced sheepishly at his friend. "Sorry, mate. I wasn't trying to look for a whale. It just happened. When a whale pops up in front of you, it's not like you can just unsee it because you have a friend who wants to see it first."

"I know. I'm happy for you. If someone else was going to be the first person in recorded history to spot a whale in Weymouth Bay, then I'm glad it was you. Could you email me a copy?"

"I will, and thanks. There was one other thing. We found a Coast Guard rescue raft floating around with no one in it. We towed it back to the beach and called the Coast Guard to let them know where it was. They came and picked it up about an hour later." James reached into his pocket and pulled out a battery. "I found this on the floor of the raft. The man from the Coast Guard said it looked like a drone battery and that I could keep it if I knew anyone who could use it."

James passed the battery to Harvey, who instantly recognized it as the drained one he'd removed from his drone the night before. He must have set it on the floor of the raft and forgotten about it.

James caught the surprised look on Harvey's face. "Is it *yours*?" he asked.

Harvey didn't answer.

A gleam came into James's eye like a light had just gone on. "It *is* yours, isn't it? It was your drone light that I saw last night bobbing up and down, and you slept so late because you were up all night, and the prime minister came to your house to congratulate you...not because she had an issue with her clothes!"

Harvey didn't say anything. He knew he wasn't supposed to talk about it to anyone.

"Seriously, mate. It's obvious from your facial expression that I'm right."

Harvey smiled. He knew he could trust James, and he simply had to share his story with someone or he would burst. "You're right about everything. The battery, the drone, and the prime minister's visit to our house."

"Why didn't you tell me? Why did you lie to me about your mum and the clothes?"

"I'm not supposed to tell anyone what happened, for security reasons. Technically, I didn't tell you because you figured it out, and I didn't lie because while the prime minister was thanking me I threw up all over her, and obviously she needed a change of clothes after that."

"You puked on the prime minister! That's insane! I can't wait to tell everyone at school."

"You can't tell. You mustn't tell. It has to be kept top secret. Kim Wilberforce told me that I needed to keep it all hush-hush for my own safety. She said it could put me in danger if it got out."

"Okay, you have my word. But what was that about MI5? On the news, it said there was a possible link between the security expert and MI5. I'm guessing they got that wrong, since you aren't, to the best of my knowledge, some type of MI5 operative."

"Yeah, you know what the media are like," Harvey shrugged. "They get things wrong all the time."

★ ★ ★

The boys spent the next hour talking about the events of the night before. They ended their conversation by trying to impress each other with vivid descriptions of their recent illnesses in ways only eleven-year-old boys can, but nothing James had experienced could trump Harvey's story about throwing up on the prime minister.

"You have an amazing story to tell," concluded James. "It's a classic adventure story. Except there were no tunnels involved."

"Tunnels?"

"Almost all adventure stories have tunnels."

"I suppose a submarine is a small floating tunnel."

"No, it isn't. Submarines are not small floating tunnels."

"Well, I think they are. And besides, I've got a gut feeling there's going to be more to this story. Who knows? Maybe there will be a tunnel involved before it's over."

Chapter 35

NO TOMATOES, PLEASE

That afternoon, the Ranger family all gathered around the TV to watch the news. It was mostly about the recovery of the Crown Jewels. Fortunately, there was no mention of Harvey or a drone. When the prime minister appeared on the TV, Harvey said, "Look, Mum. She's still wearing your clothes."

After the prime minister had finished thanking everyone who'd played a role in recovering most of the Crown Jewels, a reporter made a comment. "Prime Minister, you look very nice today in your coordinated jacket and trousers."

"Thank you," the prime minister responded. "In Weymouth this morning, I had a wardrobe incident and needed some assistance. Fortunately, I was able to get help from a wonderful wardrobe consultant in the area."

"Mum, you're almost famous," Harvey commented.

"Let's hope it doesn't go any further than that," said Mrs Ranger. "Almost famous is famous enough for me."

The reporter continued. "There has been a lot of drama in the past twenty-four hours. How would you describe the day?"

"That's a good question." Kim Wilberforce paused for a second as if searching her mind for the right words. She smiled at the reporter. "Today has been an epic adventure." And with that, she turned away from the camera, walking towards a large black car.

"Look!" Sally cried, pointing at the TV. "See that bright red blob in the prime minister's hand?"

"Oh yes! She's still got the slime you gave her, sweetie," Mrs Ranger said. "She must have had a stressful day."

* * *

The doorbell rang for a third time shortly after the TV was turned off. Harvey raced Sally to see who was there. It was Mrs Bavard, who assisted Mr Ranger at Auntie Bunny's. She ran the bakery by herself on Saturdays or when Mr Ranger was away painting watercolours. The bakery was closed on Sunday, so Mrs Bavard would box up anything that might spoil and give most of the food to the homeless centre where Mrs Ranger volunteered. The homeless centre wasn't the only stop on her route. She always dropped off a few treats for the Ranger children.

Unfortunately, Mrs Bavard was a bit of a talker, and she liked to complain about anything and everything. "Some people just like to complain," Mr Ranger would explain. "It's her thing." Once Mrs Bavard had engaged you in conversation, it was difficult to get away. Talking to her put Harvey's good listening skills to the test. He wished he had let Sally win the race to the door.

"Good to see you are up and at 'em, Harvey!" Mrs Bavard trilled. "I've brought you your Saturday treats." She passed a box to Harvey. "Here ya go. Don't eat them all at once, especially with your sensitive stomach."

"Thank you, Mrs Bavard," said Harvey, "and enjoy the rest of your day!" He hoped that would be the end of the conversation.

"I hope I do," she responded, "because this morning was a nightmare. There were police and media people coming in constantly. I was run ragged. Not sure what your father was doing, but it would have been nice to have had some extra help. Fortunately for me, my husband was able to lend a hand. By one o'clock, the place was almost dead. But that didn't stop one customer knocking over a display and another complaining about the guest Wi-Fi. He was entering the password incorrectly. How hard is it to type *flapjack*? And then there was the..."

Harvey's eyes started to glaze over as Mrs Bavard droned on with complaints about various customers and their antics. He tried to maintain eye contact, but his mind was plotting an exit strategy. Suddenly, something she said about a customer with a tomato allergy grabbed his attention.

"Sorry," he said. "Could you repeat that bit?"

"What? The bit about the tomato allergy?"

"Yes please," said Harvey.

Mrs Bavard was caught off guard. She wasn't used to being asked to repeat something and was delighted that Harvey was showing an interest.

"A man came in just before closing," she continued. "He ordered four roast beef sandwiches. He said that one was to have a hint of Marmite and two slices of pickle. He had this pompous attitude and acted like he was the King of England. When I passed him the sandwiches, he claimed that he'd asked for the Marmite and pickle one to be made with no tomatoes. Well, I either hadn't heard him or I must have forgotten. Anyway, I took the sandwich back and removed the tomatoes. But 'Oh no no, goodness gracious no! That won't do at all,' he said and insisted I make it again. I Ic said the sandwich was for a person who was allergic to tomatoes and there would still be tomato residue on the sandwich. I made it again, but I can tell you, I wasn't happy about it."

"What did he look like?" asked Harvey excitedly.

"He had a nose like Julius Caesar, a large chin, and a bald head that looked like it had been freshly shaved. When I passed him the sandwich with no tomatoes, he leaned forward a bit and peered at me over the top of his round sunglasses. What kind of hoity-toity person wears sunglasses indoors on an overcast day? Anyhow, it was then that I noticed something unique about his eyes: they were two different colours." She paused for a breath while studying Harvey's face. "Are you alright? You don't look well. Maybe you should go and lie down again. I'll say my goodbye now. You take it easy this afternoon, young man."

"Yes. I should go now. Thanks again, Mrs Bavard."

Harvey watched as Mrs Bavard went back to her car, then he quickly closed the door and rushed back to the living room. Mr Ranger was still sitting on the couch reading on his mobile. "Guess what Dad?" he said, excitedly. "Smelliwig was at Auntie's this afternoon, and he ordered a no-tomato sandwich from Mrs Bavard! And he's shaved his head!"

"Slow down, Harvey," his dad replied. "Tell me everything she said, right from the beginning.

Harvey repeated all that Mrs Bavard had told him. "So you see, it must have been Smelliwig, and that means he is with Yeoman Nick–unless there's someone else in his gang who is allergic to tomatoes and likes their sandwiches with Marmite and two slices of pickle."

"Yes, I see," said Mr Ranger. "You're probably right about that. What we still don't know is whether or not Yeoman Nick is being held against his will. This doesn't look good for him, though. Kidnappers don't usually care so much about the details of their kidnappee's sandwich preferences. Smelliwig–I must confess I feel a little silly every time I say that name–is obviously still in the area."

"Where do you think he got that name, Dad? Does he wear a wig that smells?"

"Maybe. More likely a childhood nickname that he can't shake. I'm guessing no one actually calls him that to his face, although if he's just shaved his head he'll most likely start to wear wigs and other disguises. He's going to have to fly under the radar for a bit."

"How will he do that?"

"Well, he's not going to want to move around much. And he's going to need cash. Using anything else would be traceable. He's believed to be quite wealthy, but he might not actually have much cash in hand. That could make things interesting."

"So what will he do next? How will he get cash?"

"Maybe rob a bank or two. We're just going to have to wait and see. This is a game of patience."

"I want to be the one who catches him."

"I bet you'd love that. But don't get your hopes up, Harvey. The odds of that happening are pretty slim."

"About the same as the odds of me spotting the submarine last night?"

"You've got a good point. Now, if you'll excuse me, I need to go and make some phone calls."

Harvey was feeling quite a bit better now. He sat down on the couch and opened the box from Mrs Bavard. *Let's see. Maybe I'll start with a piece of chocolate fudge cake.*

ABOUT THE AUTHOR

Stephen W. Saint is the author of numerous short stories, most of which received a grade of B- or C+. Steve is easily distracted and finds it difficult to apply himself. When he was seven, a teacher threatened to put a bomb under his chair to help him focus. The same

Photography by Shane Pegg

teacher told him he needed to pull up his socks. Surprisingly, the teacher got angry when Steve reached down and pulled them up (teachers can be unpredictable, but most are pretty great). It took nearly six years for Steve to write *Harvey Ranger: The Whale that Wasn't*. Given his short attention span, you might be surprised that he wrote the book at all. However, when you understand that the book itself was a distraction from what he was *actually* supposed to be doing (real work that pays the bills), it makes more sense.

Although he was born and now lives in Canada, Steve's childhood was spent in Weymouth and Farnham, England. He attended high school in Belleville, Ontario, Canada, before moving west to the University of Waterloo, where he majored in Applied Physics. Applied Physics didn't agree with him (he didn't apply himself), so he completed his degree with a B.Sc in General Science instead.

Steve has made a living working as a newspaper deliverer, ice cream purveyor, cook, lifeguard, remote sensing analyst, skid test technician, forklift driver, photographer, wholesale photo finishing salesman, delivery driver, research assistant, landlord, and information technology consultant. If you buy this book, he will be able to add "author" to the list.

Steve was inspired to start the Harvey Ranger books from a series of bedtime stories he created for his daughters. Picture books have the fewest number of words, so he decided to start there. The initial picture book transcript was turned down by all the publishers he sent it to (a grand total of one), so instead he decided to write a short story and then a less short story and finally a longer story.

When he isn't working or writing, Steve spends his time walking, cycling, boating, coaching soccer, geocaching, ping ponging, parenting, and engaging in church activities. At the time of writing, his favourite food is Swiss cheese and his favourite word is *pamplemousse*.

Printed in Great Britain
by Amazon

78297166R10140